tycoon

new york times *bestselling author*

katy evans

First paperback edition: June 2017

Cover design by Sara Hansen at Okay Creations
Cover image by Wong Sim
Cover model Chad Hurst
Interior formatting by JT Formatting

10 9 8 7 6 5 4 2 1

Library of Congress Cataloguing-in-Publication Data is available

ISBN-13: 978-1545501702
ISBN-13: (ebook) 978-0-9972636-5-7

table of contents

To *what if...*

playlist

"Who Knew" by Pink

"Better Than Me" by Hinder

"Everything Has Changed"
by Taylor Swift and Ed Sheeran

"Climax" by Usher

"Let Me Hold You (Turn Me On)"
by Cheat Codes and Dante Klein

"Show Me What I'm Looking For"
by Carolina Liar

"Alone Together" by Frat Out Boy

"Under Control" by Calvin Harris and Alesso

"Every Breaking Wave" by U2

"Say You Won't Let Go" by James Arthur

"One" by U2

the call

Bryn

t's a project that my parents would be proud of; that *I'm* proud of. I don't get why nobody else sees the potential. Why the bankers won't take my calls after a pitch. Or why my friend Jensen is the fifth person I've had to beg to get a meeting with the most powerful investor in the city—my last chance to convince someone my idea is good enough to fund.

There have been so many NO's, that when my phone rings late that evening and I see Jensen's number blink on my screen, I almost can't bear to hear it another time.

It takes me a few seconds, and a great pull of breath, to gather the courage to pick up and croak, "Yes?"

"Bryn, baby," Jensen says.

I hold my breath and clutch my cell a little tighter, my stomach in knots because I dread his most likely next words. That the investor I'm dying to see told Jensen that there is *no way in hell he will*—

"You got it. Tomorrow. His place at 8 p.m. Don't be late. He doesn't usually see anyone outside the office but it's the only time he could squeeze you in."

It takes me a moment to grasp what he is saying. "Ohmigod! Jensen, *thank you!*"

"No worries, post me," he says with a little chuckle.

"I will," I promise before hanging up. I throw my cell phone on the bed, and then I follow, grabbing my pillow and clutching it to my chest as I roll to my back.

Holy shit! It's on, baby.

I'm not sure my friend Jensen knows how grateful I am, but I would've squeezed the breath out of him if we hadn't been speaking on the phone.

Finally.

I've got a meeting. With *him.*

The legend. The guy with the Midas touch, and the golden eyes to match.

I fall asleep with a bundle of nerves in my stomach, tossing and turning in bed as I wonder what this man will see in me...what he will say about my project.

I spend the entire next day re-writing my pitch to be sure that I get it right. I wish that Sara, my roommate, wasn't working all day because I have no one to practice with. Talking to myself in the mirror doesn't have the same punch when I've heard the pitch a thousand times in my mind already.

Nerves accompany me as I take the train to the Upper East Side. I check the address Jensen sent me, exhaling as I wait for my stop.

I'm fully aware that this meeting can go one of four ways.

He'll give me the money.

He'll give me only part of the money.

He won't give me the money. And back to point c.), I'll realize that I have run out of options and I'm supremely royally fucked. I'll have to realize that I was dreaming and that this project sucks as much as everybody claims it does (everybody but me), or I'll have to...well, I don't know how I can get this project off the ground without any money. So, back to being fucked.

It's not like I can go back to Toasts and Bagels. They made it very clear I was the worst waitress in the world. Always "daydreaming". Forever fired.

But enough pessimism. I still have option a.) He'll give me the money. He's supposed to be a big risk taker and he takes companies no banks will touch, and no sane person would look at, and he explodes them. He takes them to the stratosphere. Okay...I admit I don't believe it, but I'm desperate. When I heard his name, and recognized it, I decided it wouldn't hurt. I mean, what other option do I have? The four options I listed involve needing someone to invest in my business, and the bankers don't want to see my face anymore.

As I ride the train to the address I was given, I'm uncomfortably warm in my jacket. Perspiration clings to my forehead, between my breasts, and pops up on my palms. Relax, Bryn. You won't cause a good impression sweating and panting.

Checking my texts through my cracked phone screen, I reread my best friend's message in reply to the text I sent her last night.

I'm completely uninspired without you here

Becka is a starving artist/writer poet. She's not really really starving but, you know what I mean. She's waiting for a big break. I suppose we all are.

Miss you too, Becks! I text back. *But I've got THE appointment!*

OMG! Go get your money honey. Dazzle him so he won't stand a chance, but then you always did dazzle that guy

Totally not true. But I'll post you.

I hop off the train and walk several walks to his building.

It's a brownstone in Park Avenue, one of the most elite of the elite spaces in town.

My lungs feel a little bit overworked from awe as I head up the steps to the double doors, grateful that I came dressed to kill in a little black dress, a jacket, and pumps. Simple, but effective.

See, I may be *feeling* a little awkward, but at least I don't *look* it.

I'm greeted by his maid. She's dressed in black and white, her hair drawn back in a neat bun, her expression stoic and formal as she leads me down the hall to a gorgeous study.

I catch my breath when I notice all the books and shelves.

It's like a reader's paradise in here. There's a sleek chrome bar, a modern mahogany glass-topped desk, and two huge whiskey-colored leather chairs that almost swallow me up when I'm instructed to wait in one.

I drum my fingers, inhaling the scent of leather and wine, remembering a guy I knew with his mechanic navy-blue uniform, black streaks on his jaw, his big nose always the first thing you'd see, which was a pity because he had beautiful eyes and a really sinful pair of lips.

He's living in luxury now. Wow. *Good* for him.

I hear footsteps approaching and the little hair on my arms prick at attention. My head turns as a tall, dark figure steps into the room, and the most intimidating guy I've ever seen enters and crosses the room toward the desk. He walks like he's the shit...his strides proud and composed, elegant and powerful.

Christos, I hear myself breathe in surprise.

He's so tall now...six three, at least. Dirty-blonde hair, gold-green eyes, chiseled jaw, and a gorgeous profile.

All in black, he looks very much a New Yorker.

He's wearing a black jacket, black pants, and a black turtleneck beneath the jacket...

I stare at him, my jaw hanging a little bit open. The man is...all man. Testosterone. Muscles. Height. Width. My chest hurts all of a sudden because I realize...

The boy you knew is gone.

I force myself to stand. "Thank you for seeing me."

He heads to the bar to pour two drinks, then he prowls over, takes the whiskey leather chair across from mine and leans forward, pushing a glass of cognac with one finger across a small table, toward me.

And he waits.

In silence.

But my stomach dips as if he'd said something ultra-sexy and decadent.

"You might not remember me, I'm sorry to be reaching out like this," I say, nervous.

"What do you want?"

There's a pleasant shiver as he speaks. Recognition of his voice, even though it's far deeper than I remember.

"I was told you sometimes invest in startups."

"I'd say more than sometimes." He raises his eyebrows as if I should've done my homework better.

Ugh, Bryn! Focus! Be SMART! Make yourself and your business irresistible! A silence settles as he eyes me, slowly setting his drink down as he leans forward and finally, unexpectedly, *smiles*. At me.

It's just a smile.

But the world tilts under its impact.

"Hello, little bit." Amusement touches his gaze as he tilts his head and watches me. "You know, I'd think you'd have grown up the ten-plus years since I last saw you. At least an inch." He leans back in his seat, seemingly displeased. Wow, this guy is not the lanky kid I knew once. This guy oozes danger.

Every ounce of "boy" is gone. *Oh God.* For a moment I wish that we could go back in time and I could discuss my startup with the guy I knew before.

But time travel is not really my talent, and it seems like I have yet to see if I even have any special talents at all— depending on what *this* guy thinks.

"I grew two in width," I shock myself saying.

He laughs then, his eyes drinking me in openly.

"Shame on you, you're not trying to see if it's true?" I ask him, frowning now.

He shrugs casually, his lips curved at the corners. "I can't help it. Something has to have changed."

"Why?"

"Because nothing good ever lasts. Even you, little bit." A smile touches those unforgettable gold-green eyes.

A shiver runs through me. Because...

Christos *recognized* me.

"I can tell you're as incorrigible as ever." I shake my head, but I'm smiling, truly just relieved that he recognized me.

"I try to be," he purrs dangerously.

I'm feeling warm all of a sudden. I can't believe I'm staring at him so much, but it's like I cannot take my eyes away. He looks achingly familiar, but at the same time, so different I cannot help but stare and track the differences in his features. The way his jaw squared out even more, the way his body filled out with hard, lean muscles that shift and ripple beneath his expensive designer clothes. I cannot believe that this is a guy I knew once.

He seems to silently be taking in my changes too, his keen stare allowing me to see that he seems to approve of it all. Even the dress I'm wearing. "You changed enough for the both of us," I blurt.

"Really. How so?" he asks.

"You grew into your nose."

"Really?" He chuckles as if despite himself.

"Width and height too. Quite a bit," I add.

"Anything else," he prods, one eyebrow rising.

"You learned how to dress."

He looks down at his black suit. "This old thing?" He grins, then shifts forward, sobering up. "What can I do for you,

Bryn? Considering I'm rather surprised to see you here, I'm eager for you to satiate my curiosity." His stare becomes keen.

"So am I. I didn't expect to be here," I admit, and for a moment when I look into his eyes, all I see is someone I've seen before. Someone who belonged in my life long ago. "You know when you had that misplaced crush on me and told me one day I'd know what it felt like to throw pebbles at someone's window wanting them to open? I'm sort of throwing rocks here."

"Not to sing me a love song," he says flatly, his eyes shuttering.

"No. Well, you know that was never...I mean..." Don't bring up your rejection of him, Bryn! "It's for something better. Business."

"Go on."

"I knew that'd get you." I smile privately. "So it's true your love is money now."

"She gives back what I put in. Though her ass isn't as juicy as I like," he says nonchalantly.

"Wow. No matter how polished you look, your mouth is still as crude as ever."

"Thank you," he purrs, his eyes grinning at me.

I laugh. Then I sober up and realize he's waiting for me to speak. "I'm looking for money for my startup," I say.

"How much."

"One hundred thousand."

"I don't invest less than a million." He twirls his whiskey in his glass, eyeing the liquid.

"Well then, I'll ask for a million."

He raises his brows, setting his glass down. "It's not how much you want to ask for, it's how much the company's worth." Eyebrows up, he skewers me with a cold, intimidating look.

"It'll be worth more than a million, trust me," I bluff.

"Good for you. Except…" he leans back with a rustle of clothes, every athletic inch of his black-clad body flowing sinuously like a feline with the move, "considering that has yet to happen and I'll need to trust you on that, my trust needs to be earned."

This version of Christos is even more intimidating than the old one, unfortunately.

I try to hide it, keeping my voice as level as possible. "How does one earn your trust?"

"I'd tell you if I were interested, but I'm not exactly sure that I am." He eyes me as if debating in silence.

This guy is the only guy in the world that unnerves me in this way, and I can't seem to slow the fast pounding of my heart in my chest as I try to remember what I came here to say.

"I have a full presentation for you. I'm not taking no for an answer." I reach into my briefcase.

"Darling. Are you ready?"

I start at the female voice and glance at a gorgeous woman striding into the study. Christos continues looking at me as he stands and reaches for the cell phone the woman extends out.

"We're done here," he answers her as he pockets the phone, his gaze remaining on me.

"I'll wait for you in the car." She leans up and kisses his jaw, her hands proprietary on his chest, then sends me a woman-to-woman claiming look, before she swishes away, all glittering jewels and lean body.

There's a silence as he approaches, and for a second all I can hear is the sound of a toilet flushing, taking my only opportunity with a possible investor away.

"I'll think about it," he says.

"Christos."

"I said I'll think about it," he says from the door.

"Please do," I say as he exits the room. I cup the sides of my mouth, "I'll be back tomorrow. Same time?" I say jokingly.

I'm surprised when I hear footsteps returning. He pauses when our eyes meet. "I'll make contact," he says, raising his eyebrows meaningfully, "If I'm interested in hearing more." He nods. "Nice to see you, Bryn."

"Nice to see you. Christos."

Well, that went sort of awful.

No, it went beyond awful. I head out of his brownstone and am so stressed about how bad it went that, rather than head straight to my flat, I walk along the Upper East Side because...well, it's something I do. Walking. It helps me think.

But I'm so mind-fucked right now I can't really think at all.

There's a heavy feeling in my chest, a tight little knot in my stomach, and I can't seem to get past the moment Christos walked into the room and...was *there*. In the same space. After all these years wondering... just wondering. *Endlessly*. About him.

He was a little aloof, a little playful, and a little too...

Sexy, a little voice whispers.

And he still has that pull on you, girl.

I push that scary little thought aside, but I can't stop thinking about Aaric.

Aaric freaking Christos.

It's like Erick, pronounced similarly, but with an A at the beginning. The first letter of the alphabet, double in dose. You could say that describes the man perfectly. We met in high school, and he was always more than anyone could handle.

Considering how difficult it's been to get an appointment with him, that seems to continue to be the case.

He was always...more. More than the norm, always the first. The first you'd see in a room. The first who'd dare the dares in the parties that no one else would. The first to offer help when you needed it, but also the first to sneer when you fucked up.

He called me Lips. And "little bit".

And he wanted me.

I wasn't interested (at least, I never admitted to myself that I *was*). He left the city with his brother a few years after we met. And that was that.

So this meeting was a bit of a wildcard. I didn't know if he'd remember me, if he'd ever thought about me after he left.

Twelve years is a long time, after all.

I've heard rumors about him from old school friends, Jensen included (who kept in touch with him when he left). I've heard of how much he has changed, how merciless and cold and threatening he has become—no longer the easygoing guy he used to be. It's not like he's involved in shady business—but he's definitely a name that seems to inspire chills in other men.

Even then, everyone wants him to consider investing in their startups. He only considers risky ventures, ventures the banks won't touch. To be denied by Christos means your options are gone—and you're basically fucked.

I really don't want to be fucked.

But seeing him tonight, all-powerful and larger-than-life, I'm thinking I may be in way over my head here. Playing with the big boys in a business-game that I'm not sure I know how to play.

Christos has clearly gone on with his life. He's filthy rich, has a gorgeous girlfriend who calls him darling, and is some Manhattan hotshot. Me? My life is worse than it was when I was seventeen and in high school. After his mother died and he left my life, it's like the sun left with him. One tragedy after another. I've been grappling to find my footing ever since.

I've been sad, trying to figure out how and *what* could fill the hole and give my life meaning.

It means something to me. My startup. It's what I'm good at and what keeps me connected to my mom and dad. It's also what I've grown to love.

I'm thirty years old and this December, I'll be thirty-one. I thought I'd be married and successful by this age. I'm neither. I've made peace with the things that don't pan out as planned, but I've also still got dreams and moving to New York was my first step to prove how serious I am about them. The first step needed to make them come true.

When I get to my small flat and realize my roommate Sara isn't home yet, I sit down on my bed with some of my plans and sketches. The only thing that makes me feel good is getting lost in my own little world. But as I grab my drawing pens, I can't seem to focus.

I pull out my laptop, boot it up, and open the web browser.

I search *Aaric Christos girlfriend*.

Miranda Santorini comes up. She's a Manhattan socialite. They've been seen together for the past three months. Her dad owns real estate Christos is after, some speculate.

I'm about to shut my computer when I hear Sara's voice. "What are you looking at? Is that, *whoa*, lady boner alert—is that Aaric *Christos?*"

I shut my laptop and turn. Sara put out an ad the week I arrived in Manhattan, I answered, we hit it off, and we've been rooming together ever since. Younger than me by two years, she's tall and skinny, a ballerina with a broken ankle and a heart of gold, she works as a concierge at a four-star hotel Downtown. I'm surprised that she knows who he is. "How do you know him?"

"Everyone knows him. He's lava."

I groan despairingly. "He's the whole volcano."

"How do *you* know him?" she asks.

"He's an old acquaintance. I saw him tonight." I rub my temples, which are starting to throb from the pressure of re-membering our meeting. "He looked really good. He's like McDreamy—better as he matures. God, he looked so confi-dent. Successful. Like he's at the very pinnacle."

"Newsflash, he *is*. He's huge around here." She eyes me from the door. "Is that a banging look?" she asks mischievous-ly.

I flush and glance at my shut laptop. "Come on. He's got a girlfriend."

She wags her brows. "You still want to bang him."

"No! It's just...he was this boy I used to know. It's...I don't know. He's the biggest *what if* I've ever had in my life. The one you always wonder about."

"I can't believe you knew Christos." She walks to my bed and drops down on it, kicking her shoes off and curling her legs beneath her as she sits.

"Me either. He wanted me for a time, I guess. I never could go for it," I say, shaking my head. "I've always regretted it. I went to talk to him about business tonight, but it didn't go well."

"He's probably thinking if you didn't give him a chance, why should he give you one now?"

"Maybe," I agree, but I shake my head. "He doesn't even know what I'm selling yet."

"Find a way to see him again. Find a way to get him to say yes."

"You know what?" I gather my laptop and shoot her a playful, chiding look. "Go and do your stuff, let me have my pity party."

She laughs and raps her knuckles to the wall behind my bed. "I'm right behind this wall if you need me."

I nod, then I grab my papers and pens. "How did your audition go?" I ask as she heads for the door.

"As good as your meeting."

"Oh no," I groan, raising my voice as she walks out. "You'll get the part next time!"

"You'll get the guy."

"No. I'm not after the guy, Sara. I'm after money for my startup."

"Then he'll show you the money," she yells from the hall.

"You had me at hello!" I yell back.

I'm determined for him to see I'm not ashamed to throw more than rocks at his window. I'll throw the whole bucket next time we meet.

favor

Christos
18 hours ago...

I smash the ball into the wall, nearly hitting Wells. "You get the ring?" he asks.

"Yep." I smash it again.

"You're really doing it?"

I shrug. "Why not?" I turn and smash. Smash, smash.

"Business as usual?" he asks.

I head over for water, guzzle some down, and head back. Bounce the ball, smash. "We're friends. We have fun together. We respect each other. She's willing for us to have an open marriage. She gets my money. I get respect."

"Damn right!" he says.

"Christos." I hear a voice behind me.

"Hill." I greet Jensen, an old high school friend who is leaning on the glass door with his racket at his side.

"Thirty seconds?" he says.

I head over, wipe my sweat with a towel.

"I've got a favor. I know someone who's been trying to get a meeting with you for weeks."

"I'm really busy." I toss the towel at a nearby basket.

"Yeah. *Understatement.*" He grins—a pause as he waits for me. "You think you can see her?"

"I'm sorry, I really *am* busy." I smile and slap his back.

"Come on, it's a special friend of mine. She wants your Midas touch on her startup. She's your friend too."

I arch a brow.

"Bryn Kelly. Remember her? Five feet tall. A little funny—"

"I know Bryn," I cut him off.

"So will you see her?"

Bryn Kelly.

You look like a guy who thinks he'll get to kiss me.

I will.

I push the thought out of my mind, unaware of how long I've been silent.

A restless sensation grips me, and I scrape my jaw with my hand as I try to shake it aside. "My place tomorrow at 8. I'll fit her in between changing and leaving for a thing with Miranda."

"Owe you." He winks. "Let's do dinner next weekend."

I lift my racket in consent as I walk away, grab the ball, and smash it against the wall so hard the glass enclosure rattles.

serendipity

Bryn

I t's Saturday evening, and I found a dog-walking stint to help pay my rent while I get my startup going. From noon to evening, I have a great time walking a group of small dogs, and three large dogs, separately. I end up soaked in sweat and distracted from my business worries, thankfully.

Once I take the last dog home, a retriever named Milly, I get a gym coupon along with my payment from Mrs. Ford. May as well give it a shot, so I check out the new gym and get some stretching in before I take a shower and head out to hunt something to eat before I head home.

I'm craving a salad from one of my favorite Tribeca markets. It has the most delicious balsamic dressing and lettuce that always has a perfect fresh crunch. The combination of berries with goat cheese always gets me. I'm easy like that.

I call Jensen, but get his voicemail.

"Hey. I need another appointment and I need it to be more than five seconds long. Stop ignoring my calls. I'm not backing out now!"

Frustration eats at me. I hang up and sigh.

I walk a couple more blocks into Tribeca and notice a sleek black car slow to a stop at the end of the block. A young couple exits the car, while another couple waiting on the sidewalk steps up to greet them. They're all dressed to the nines—the women in skirts and silk tops, the men in slacks and button shirts.

It takes me less than a second to recognize the tallest among the men.

Yeah.

The broad-shouldered

Tall

Utterly dark

Dirty-blond

Handsome

Extremely hot

one.

I slow down my pace.

Swallowing back my disbelief, I pull out my earbuds and tuck my phone into my bag, my hand trembling slightly. I can't believe it's him. Is the universe finally getting in on my plan? What do I do now, walk and talk business?

There's no way I can do that.

But it's not like I can cross the street and avoid them, that would be infantile and obvious. I continue walking, my head canted down.

I peek up and see the four of them are on the sidewalk under a restaurant awning, talking.

The beat of my heart accelerates the closer I get. Aaric the boy would have made me feel safe, but Aaric the man makes me feel like a fish on a hook.

Well, fuck *that*, if we're going to be in business I can't pay attention to my heart. I inhale and prepare to walk past when I hear—

"Long time no see."

It's Christos's low, deep voice. My heart stops, then restarts with a pounding racket in my head.

I turn my head, smiling as I do.

"Well, if it isn't my future business partner. I was just thinking of you," I say.

He leans over to greet me with a brush of his lips on my cheek. "I'm sure all your thoughts of me color your face pink like that."

The touch makes me tingly and uncomfortable and hot. Hot all over.

I widen my eyes.

Is he seriously flirting with me in front of his girlfriend?

What's the deal with him?

"Bryn? Is that you? It's been forever since I've seen you. Come here!" Aaric's brother, Cole, says as he pulls me into a hug.

"Cole!" I say, hugging my old high school friend back. "Are you living here with your brother?"

"Not with him—but I'm definitely a resident," he concedes.

After greeting the women—Miranda, Aaric's blonde, who greets me coolly and looks down her nose at me, and Gwen, Cole's blonde, who doesn't bother to look me in the eye—I search for something to say as all four pairs of eyes examine me with interest.

"I never expected to see you again." I look at Aaric as I speak. Silently asking—*are you willing to see me again or what, you stubborn man?*

He stares down at me, taking in my face, his expression unreadable but his eyes intense as he drinks me in.

"We're getting drinks, do you want to accompany us, Bryn?" Cole asks.

Hesitation grips me. "Oh, I'd hate to be a fifth wheel," I hedge.

The women don't look pleased about Cole's invitation.

Especially Christos's blonde.

"That term doesn't exist between old friends. Come on. I'm sure my brother here would love to catch up with his Lips."

Aaric shoots his brother an icy look that makes my heart skip a beat, and the women purse their lips in jealousy.

Christos meets my gaze and motions toward the restaurant door. I follow him. He towers over me as I step through the door he holds open for me. I can smell him. He smells different. More...dangerous.

Familiar but new.

We shuffle inside, and the maître d' appears. "Mr. Christos, a pleasure as always. Your table is ready."

"We'll be five tonight, David," he requests.

"Oh, of course! One minute." The man hustles to accommodate him.

"Are you certain?" I ask out loud.

"Completely," Cole answers.

But when my face still shows doubt, Christos turns and says, "I insist." His eyes meet mine, and as they do, a subtle electric current passes through me.

"So are you two friends?" Christos's date asks a bit snottily.

"High school," Christos says as we wait to be led to our table.

I edge closer to Cole and push onto my tiptoes. "She's beautiful. Is that why he likes her? She's like *model* beautiful," I say, trying to keep my voice low.

He leans over, laughter in his voice as he nods with mock somberness. "She swears that while God took seven days in creating the world, Aaric would've taken six." He winks as he straightens.

I realize Aaric is watching us, and as his date speaks to the other girl, I say, "Sounds like she dotes on you."

His brows shoot upwards in amusement, and though he's not smiling, his eyes begin to dance devilishly. "You two were talking about me."

Lightning fast, a warm flush runs up my face, and I quickly change the subject. "Anyway. Should I tell you about my business?" I say.

God, he's enjoying this. Isn't he?

He starts to follow the maître d' to our table, pushing his fingers into my back to urge me forward with one hand, while doing the same to his date with the other. "Not until I'm interested," he leans down to say in my ear.

"But— that doesn't even make sense." I frown and walk forward as he guides me.

"You're part of the business," he says.

"Yes. I am. What? You don't want to do business with me…your little bit?" I ask in disbelief.

He shakes his head, his tone tender but rueful. "You're not my little bit." His thumb caresses my bare back, and a host of tingles climb up my spine and neck.

"For old times' sake." He pulls out my seat, not answering. "Christos!" I hiss as he turns to his date. He helps her with her chair then takes a seat beside me.

He leans close to me. "Can you relax and enjoy yourself without talking business?"

He raises his eyebrows, challenging.

I stare at his hard male chest and his thick throat, my head spinning dizzily at his words. He's so close I can smell the soap and shampoo on his skin and hair, the cologne drifting from somewhere around him.

"Excuse me while I go freshen up in the ladies'." I inhale deeply and push away from the table.

I enter the bathroom, but instead of heading for a stall, I stop at the sink and stare at myself in the mirror.

He really pushes my buttons, this man.

Even in school. He was the first workaholic I'd ever met. Fixed everyone's phones, cars, and even sold tests. He was a little bit too bad, and I was a little bit too good. He was a demon in the making and I was still Daddy's little angel. I suppose it was my fault that we never…that…well, I just could never believe he might actually want me. Not for keeps. I was too afraid to get hurt.

I wash my hands, splash some cold water on my neck, and then head back to the table. I try not to stumble when I watch Christos lift his head from his conversation and quietly watch me return, that unreadable, dark gaze on me.

I slide into my seat while conversation continues between the women and Cole—

"—so there's this endless line of people, and I…"

Aaric's hand is curved around his wine and his thumb is stroking the glass. Up and down.

"So what brings you to the city?" Cole asks me when his date finishes with her anecdote.

"Business. I've been in town for six weeks."

"Good."

Christos moves his head closer to me and leans forward, as if to exclude the others from our conversation.

"Plan to stay?" he asks, gruffly.

I tilt my head to meet his gaze.

"I'm living in Nolita with a friend. I have a gig dog walking since waitressing is not my thing. I'm looking for an investor for my startup and was hoping you would see me again."

"Call his office," Cole interrupts.

I look up at his handsome, but less intimidating, brother and smile. "I already did."

Christos digs a hand into his suit pocket and places a sleek white-and-silver letter card before my place setting. "Call again." Christos meets my gaze and holds it, some sort of warning in his gaze.

I'm not sure what he's warning me about.

That I need to be persistent?

Or that I need to be sure that I want to do business with him?

That maybe our close proximity…

"—right, Christos? The best startups you've ever funded have always come to you unawares."

"Best things always creep up on you," he agrees.

I smile, but my smile falters when his date snuggles up to his side as if she thinks he was talking about her.

I tremble as I take his card and tuck it into my pocket.

"What happened to Kelly's, Bryn?" he asks me, once again turning to speak to me in a low voice, as if wanting to exclude everyone.

"Bankruptcy. We couldn't keep it."

He looks at me and I see concern in his eyes, but I look away because his judgement is unbearable.

If he doesn't like my idea, what will I do?

I'd always thought I'd work at the Kelly department stores.

Christos must notice how uncomfortable admitting Kelly's fall was, because the rest of the evening he engages in conversation with everyone else—no more lowering his voice for one-on-one talks with me. Even Cole sent me a sad smile but made sure to drop the subject.

By the time dinner is over, I definitely feel like a fifth wheel. A part of me wishes I were alone with Christos so I can talk to him, but another part of me feels vulnerable with him. Does he remember what it's like to hustle or has all the success taken that away?

After dinner, we step under the awning again. "Take you home?" Christos asks me as his black car pulls up to the curb. He asks me casually, but his gaze is intent, more demanding than his tone.

"Oh no, I'll walk. Thank you. Goodnight." I say my goodbyes and his possessive, protective stare burns into my back as I head down the block.

Walking to Nolita, I push in my earbuds and replay the meeting with a ball in my stomach. Christos's voice, quietly asking me, *What happened?*

I don't know why the concern in his eyes got to me, enough I thought I'd sort of lose my cool.

I'm sure he wanted to know more about what happened, and maybe even if I was okay. He could have hardly missed the news shortly after my parents' death: that our department stores defaulted and had to declare bankruptcy. They were taken over. Everyone thought I had money from my parents that I could use to recover it. I didn't. Now the Kelly stores belong to a huge conglomerate—someone who doesn't have Kelly as their last name.

It hurts to lose the store your family built so shortly after you lost your whole family. I remember how I would work in the warehouses every weekend…open the stores with my dad every morning…But despite the good memories, I know that Kelly's would have held me back in Austin, and now I have an opportunity to start something new.

I didn't really *lose* Kelly—all that I learned from it is still with me.

It's been six weeks since I arrived in New York. I've done things I've never done in my life—and I'd never have been able to come this far if it hadn't been for the hard work and dedication that my parents instilled in me when I was young. I feel confident that I'm becoming my own woman, that my life has something better in store.

I wanted to tell him that, but I was afraid my voice would betray me—and the last thing I want is Christo's pity. I want his help, but I'd die if I saw pity in his eyes. He would have hardly known that the pain in my voice would have been due to the loss of my parents, not the loss of the business they'd built. Because losing Kelly's opened up opportunities for me I'd never seen before, and I'm learning to see the loss as a blessing.

When I arrive at my apartment, I hear sniffling and I peer into the small living room and find Sara on the living room couch, her hair a mess, another mess of used tissues on the side table we use as a small coffee table. "What happened?" I ask.

"I got fired." She looks up from a tissue, her face breaks. "I had no idea they'd start making cuts and I'd be the first to go." She blows her nose and tosses the tissue down in a ball to join the others. "What am I going to do?"

I grab a wastebasket, toss in all the tissue balls and the empty box of tissues, and set a fresh box before her. "You'll get a new job." I sit down beside her.

"It's not that easy—"

"You can walk dogs with me."

"That's your gig."

"I'll split it with you. I won't be able to dedicate as much time to it as I want to—I'll be too busy working on the startup."

"Really? How are you so confident you'll get the money?"

"Because I saw him again tonight. And I'm hoping I can wear him down."

"It's not wishful thinking? Sorry to break it to you, roomie, but half of the city wants this man's backing. Everyone thinks they have a genius idea or wants someone who'll help them make their stupid idea *genius*."

"Maybe. But I still mean to wear him down." I grin, pour two cups of tea, and then hand one over to her. "You okay?"

"I don't know," she says, smiling wanly at me, as if thankful I asked. "I just can't figure out what's gone wrong with my life." She rubs the tissue along her nose and crumples it up only to get a new one. "I went to ballet school. I broke my ankle just before graduation. So with ballet no longer an option, I tried Broadway. Two years and nothing. So I become a concierge, and even then, something supposedly easy, I fail."

"You didn't fail, Sara. It wasn't your end game, it was your in-the-meantime job."

"Yeah, well." She hikes up one shoulder in a sad shrug. "I'm starting to wonder if most of us aren't destined to be stuck in our in-the-meantime."

I don't know what to say. I wonder that too. "I may agree," I say. "But then you see someone, someone who had it worse than anyone, and who made it big. Not because he got lucky—he worked for it. It makes sense that if we work hard enough, we can go somewhere too."

"You really like this guy," she says, eyes flaring as if it's just dawning on her that I really do know Christos. And like him, like she says.

"No. I mean…" I quickly interject. "I *admire* him. We were in high school when we met, and I admired his gumption. I suppose I liked him too," I finally admit, "but I could never understand how he made me feel. I guess I liked him enough that it confused me." I shake my head violently. "But enough about that. I'm excited about the startup. If this takes off and you don't have a job, I'll hire you."

"When do I start?" she smirks.

"Who knows? Call God's number and ask?" I show her Christos's card, then notice the surprise on her face and laugh.

"Give me that," she says when I pry it back.

"Over my dead BOOTY. It's my Golden Ticket and I'm not giving it up even to you. I'll give you some of my chocolate, though." I pull out the Godiva chocolate I have stashed away in my nightstand and toss it in her lap. Sara groans happily. "Do we have any ice cream?"

"Anything else?" I ask as I pull out an ice cream tub from the fridge and bring it over, along with two spoons.

"Yes. Can I adopt you?" she asks as she sits straight when I join her on the couch.

"Come on. I'm two years older than you are." I roll my eyes and we sit together, eating ice cream while she thinks of her job, and I think of Christos.

"I know what else I'm missing. Confidence. I seem to have lost it somewhere," she says, frowning thoughtfully at our silent TV screen.

"I have confidence in you," I counter.

"Good. 'Cause I have confidence in you too. Boss." She grins, the tissues forgotten.

After binging on chocolate and ice cream, I fall asleep with my laptop on my bed, my designs scattered around, and an image of Christos telling me he wants it.

double a

Christos

8 years ago…

DEPARTMENT STORE OWNERS KILLED
IN VEGAS FIRE

"Fuck." I scrape my hand down my jaw. An image of Bryn's parents comes to mind as I scan the paper. I want to punch something.

"Christos? Are you ready?" a familiar female voice asks from behind me.

I shut the paper closed. "Give me a minute."

I check on the burial time, glance at my watch and realize there's no time for me to bury my own blood, catch a flight, and be there on time for hers. But I can't put a lid on my instinct to protect her. Be there for her.

I pull out my wallet, punch in a number of a local florist, and ask for a bouquet of gardenias. Her favorite.

"The message, sir?" the attendant asks.

"Wish I were there. Love, Aaric."

"Erick?"

"Double A, R, I, C. Aaric."

"Got it."

"Love, Aaric," I repeat.

Yeah. That's not how I planned to tell her I loved her, but I go with it anyway. Today I bury someone else I never got the chance to love.

Seems stupid the way we hold back on these things now. Bryn lost her parents—the same day I lost my little girl.

I recite my credit card number, hang up, slip the card back into my wallet, and grab my leather jacket. Much like the one Bryn gave me once.

the shiny silver-embossed card

Bryn

Instead of taking me to reception, the number on Aaric's card takes me straight to a direct line that I'd never had access to before. I rush on to say, "Hello. I was calling to schedule an appointment with Mr. Christos."

"Who's calling? And would this be the youngest or eldest?"

"Eldest. Aaric. And it's Bryn Kelly."

"Ah, yes, Miss Kelly. He asked me to shuffle his schedule around if you called. If you can be here at 6, I'll get you in before he leaves the office."

Whoa.

He *did?*

My heart skips a little.

"I appreciate it. Truly. Thank you!"

Noticing it's 4:51 p.m. already, I lay out my outfit with care, do my hair, apply makeup—not a lot, but enough to make me look polished—and add my faux diamond studs from Macy's.

"Are you still up for doing some dog runs?" I ask Sara after a brief knock on her bedroom door.

She's watching TV, still in pajamas. On a Monday.

Rolling to her stomach with a groan, she lifts her head to shoot me an are-you-kidding look. "Anything to get me out of the apartment!"

"Okay—" I cross the room and hand her an address. "Mrs. Wellington is first. Her dog's name is Natchez. He's my favorite. A friendly little Husky. Take him to Washington Square Park, he likes it there. I'll call to let her know you're coming."

"Yes, boss." She leaps off the bed.

"I'm not your boss. *Yet.*" I wink.

"Trifle details." She sticks her tongue out and jogs over to her small bathroom.

After a quick call to Mrs. Wellington, I head for Brooklyn.

I wring my hands the entire train ride.

Today is the day I'm going to make my pitch, and I want him to *go* for it.

After I step off the train and walk three blocks to my destination, I check my briefcase to make sure I have everything I need.

The warehouse is just short of huge and simple on the outside. So simple, all red brick, that I find it difficult to locate the door.

I reach out to pull open the inconspicuous door when it opens on its own and a group of three young, sharp men dressed in business suits step out. One gives me a once over, mumbles something under his breath that makes the other men cackle and slap his back.

Well. I suppose I chose the right outfit.

I step in and stare in mounting amazement. Wow!! Aaric has really done well for himself. The warehouse looks unremarkable on the outside, but the moment you step inside, the edgy, state-of-the-art interior catches you off guard.

Flat TVs line the red brick walls, industrial beams grace the ceilings, and polished cement covers the floor. Yet it is the cleanliness, the equipment, the size, the museum-like quality of every finish inside that makes me realize...never doubt again.

I follow the signs and head to the first-floor bathroom to freshen up.

"I'm telling you, not even his mother could love him. He's fucking intolerable and I'm over this," one employee is telling another by the sink.

"You are not over this, you just started this job."

"He calls at 5 a.m.! He has no respect for my personal time or anyone else's."

"He pays you for every hour of your day, especially overtime hours. *Plus* that's in our contracts—oh."

They quiet when they spot me. I'm hurrying to make my appointment on time so I keep dabbing a cool, moist tissue down the back of my neck and between my breasts.

They leave. I quickly head to the stall to pee when I hear footsteps and the sound of the bathroom door slamming and frantic kissing follows.

I'm just about to head out to wash my hands when I realize a couple is making out near the bathroom sink.

Oh brother. I peer through the gap in the bathroom stall and can make out a pair of women's heels digging into a partly bared male ass as he starts pounding her. He's got a *great* ass. So great she seems to be enjoying digging into it with her slim, inked ankles and those heels.

"*Oooooh.* God yes. Did you lock the door?" the woman asks on a hushed moan.

"Of course, baby." A gruff male response, buried in her neck.

I shut my eyes with a little bit of longing because I don't even know how long it's been since I had sex, then I lean my forehead on the back of the door and suppress the urge to bang myself against it. *Ugh. Really?*

I suffer through their entire fuck and their joint orgasm.

Minutes and minutes of sighs and groans.

After they're done, I peer under the stall and watch a pair of women's heels and men's shiny gray designer shoes leave.

I step outside, fix my hair, and exhale before I leave and hurry up the stairs onto the second floor—straight to the biggest doors I can find—and direct myself to the busy PA sitting behind a Mac computer.

"I'm here to see Mr. Christos. I'm Bryn Kelly."

"Your appointment was at six."

We stare at one another.

"Yes." I widen my eyes when I realize that it's 6:21 p.m.

"Mr. Christos hates when an appointment is late," his assistant snaps.

"I'm here now. Do you suppose you could fit me in? I'm…an old acquaintance."

"He's heading out of the office. Sorry." The phone rings. The woman looks close to a panic attack as she picks up. "Yes,

Mr. Christos? Aha. Yes, I'll bring it over. I'll do that as well."
She hangs up and hurries to do his bidding.

"I'll bring him that." I take the folders she has gathered.

"You'll get me fired."

"Or promoted."

I head toward the doors.

"Miss Kelly, truly—" she objects as she chases me.

I ignore her pleas and head inside to find Christos bent over his desk, signing documents.

"Thanks," he says without looking up as he hears me come in. "And if Miss Kelly deigns herself to—"

"She's deigned to appear, sir, and she's truly sorry she's late."

His eyebrows lift for a fraction of a second. His lips part. He quickly rises to his full composure.

Our eyes hold, and his eyebrows lift a fraction more as I gape at him. Like a fool. An utter and complete fool. He's in a black suit, no tie, his hair slicked back to reveal his hot-as-sin features.

He seems to recover quickly. But I take longer. Forcing myself to move and step deeper into his office.

There's silence. He looks as intimidating as he looked at his place. He also looks vexed, his irritation evident as he takes me in without the barest hint of a smile.

His brows slant low over his eyes in a frown. "I'm sorry." He shakes his head, lips pursed, irritated and just a hint amused. "And you are?"

"I'm your next appointment. The wicked Miss Kelly."

His lips curve, but he shakes it off. He glances past my shoulders, a stern look on his features. "Make sure this doesn't happen again." He hands the papers to his assistant, who crept up behind me while I ogled him, then he shoots me a glance. "Lips, I leave in…ten minutes. I'm wrapping up."

Why am I licking my lips because he called me *lips?*

"Oh. Well then, I'll walk you to the train," I say, licking my lips yet again.

"Gym, you mean."

"Exactly. I was heading there myself."

He rakes his eyes down my body as if determining whether I work out or not. "Right." He smiles.

I purse my lips. "I'm sorry I'm late, I was detained."

He narrows his eyes.

"Can we do this again?" I propose. I go to the door and inhale and then walk back in.

"Hi," I say with fake cheer, my heart pounding nervously.

He exhales in exasperation. "We might as well get this over with." He motions for me to close the door.

"I've got ten minutes," he says.

"I ask for twenty." I shut the door.

"Ten," he growls.

"Fifteen then."

"Ten, little bit." A smile tugs his mouth, and he shakes his head in bemusement.

"Okay, eleven it is," I concede.

No longer playful, he glances nonchalantly at his watch. Taking his seat. "Nine minutes thirty now. Want to waste any more time negotiating?" His expression is unrelenting.

"Okay then! Let's start."

I pull out my notes, and I can't help but take a peek at him only to find him staring at me in silence.

He appears thoughtful, and by the crease in his forehead, terribly unhappy about something.

He looks at me, pointing at the folders. "Are you going to hold those for the remaining minutes, or do you want me to look at them?"

It's killing me, the way he smirks at me. What is he trying to do? I don't understand.

"I'm sure I want you to have a look." I extend my hand, but instead of taking them, he kicks out of his chair and approaches.

He nudges the folder open before me and leans over my shoulder. He points with his index finger to the first page. "House of Sass. That's your name for it?"

Close to my ear, his voice is rich and deep, smooth as velvet. A rasp of intrigue laces the words.

"Yes," I breathe.

I turn my head—catching his eyes. Or rather, his eyes catching *mine*.

"Hmm," he says.

He takes the folder now and brings it to his desk. He reads for a second, then he lifts his gaze to me.

I'm so nervous I could vomit.

"It makes me feel good to make people feel good, I'm selfish," I explain.

"You're not selfish." His stare is direct, eyes a deep green-gold staring into me. He moves his arm, closing the folder.

"But I'm not sure it's got enough, bit." He shakes his head, and his low words take a moment to register, because his gaze drifts to my mouth and I can't think straight.

My eyes drop to his mouth too—his unsmiling, sexy mouth. His clothes are of high quality, but there's a rawness to him that the elegant clothes cannot conceal.

It's not just his imposing frame behind his imposing desk, but also his unreadable expression that makes me want to penetrate the deliberate blankness on his face.

I swallow. I force my eyes up and say, "It's more. It would have my designs."

He leans back, smiling. "I'm listening."

Does his every move have to remind me of his sexual attractiveness?

"I'm self-taught," I explain, pulling out a few of my drawings. My favorites. Long dresses, mini-skirts, silky blouses. "I was always into clothing at Kelly's, but after my parents died and I had to make do, I started making my own clothes from what I had—people like them. People really like them."

"Hmm." He scrapes his jaw, staring at the designs then at me.

"Department stores aren't as strong as they used to be," he says.

"We can have a website. Make it cool like Shopbop and Revolve."

"What will distinguish you from them?"

Silence.

He eases out of his chair. "See, you have to know these things."

"I'm the creative mind; you're the business mind."

He stands upright in one fluid motion. He's tall, at least a head taller than me, and well built. Athletic and defined as he stands before me. His hair is combed stylishly backward atop a nose that is elegant, a face that is beautiful and masculine.

"Time's up."

"I'm not done yet."

"I didn't say we were done, I said time's up."

He heads to the end of his office and pulls out a duffel bag.

"Christos, you know you want to help me. There's potential here. It's not my startup's fault I fucked up my pitch a bit. I was flustered."

"Flustered," he repeats.

"By you and by the sex I had to endure before coming up here." I glance at his shoes, then at him, as he stares at me with quiet speculation.

"Someone was having sex in the bathroom."

"And."

"I thought it was you."

"Someone was having sex in my corporate bathroom?"

"Yes." I glance at his shoes, grateful they're black and big. Not the ones I saw earlier.

"It sure as fuck wasn't me."

"I know. I saw his shoes, and they're not your shoes."

He watches me as if I'm a little dumb. "We had an appointment at six, I was ready at six."

Gulp.

He picks up the phone on his desk and punches a number. "Get the car ready for me."

"Thank you for your time," I say, but I can't leave like this. How can I persuade him to do more for me?

He stops me at the door—as if he senses my disappointment. "I want to help you, but this is business. It's not personal, Bryn."

I swallow. "I know."

Fuck. He hated it.

I'm happy for him, he's on top of the world. Nobody deserves it more. I'm happy for him, but there's this restless feeling inside me, one that appeared when she called him darling, one that won't go away. *You had your chance, you lost it,* I tell myself. Never mind I was young and stupid, and very scared. We weren't meant to be, maybe casual acquaintances...not more.

"I've busted my ass too hard to risk my neck for a vaguely conceived startup."

"It's not vaguely conceived."

"You need more here."

"I'll have more!"

"You need to bring it."

He motions for me to follow him, and I do. He leads us to a private elevator and punches the down arrow, and when we step inside, we face off for a moment.

The space is confined—and his scent is everywhere. It reminds me of my childhood, of the younger version of me. Having him standing so near in such a closed space makes him impossible to ignore. He's in front of me, behind me, above me, and below me, all at once.

There's an odd little tug from his body to mine, as if there's a force trying to lure me closer to him, a magnetism in him that's primal and animalistic. He's standing close and yet instead of feeling invaded, like I should, I am achingly aware of how many inches still separate us. How many inches still stand between me and his large, hard, warm body, a wall of muscle and elegance before me.

I try to ignore it. I'm not after him to get laid. I had my chance—I said no.

I ball up the yearning and try to pretend he's not as magnetic as he is. Try to pretend he's just a wall. Or basically an ATM. The only ATM that can finance my baby.

But no.

He's more than that.

Among the most memorable—he was the guy who gave me his jacket one awful, awful day when I got my period early and stained my stupid shorts. People were snickering. I didn't know why. One of my friends told me. I wanted to cry. Christos took off his jacket and handed it to me silently. He didn't snicker like everyone else. I tied it around my waist, hurried to my car, and drove home in tears.

I could never give him his jacket back. It would have been too embarrassing for him to think it had gotten stained with my *period blood*. Guys are funny about those things.

So I bought him a new jacket. Leather, the best. He was lean, but he had broad shoulders, so I bought him a medium. It wouldn't fit him now. It cost me a fortune. The one he's wearing now would cost ten times as much.

But it didn't matter. He was different then.

His dad was gone and his mom was sick, so he never seemed quite as young as his age said he should be. He always acted older. More worldly, maybe even a little more jaded.

I could probably play the crying card with him and bend him to my will, but I won't because that's cheating. And because if it fails, I'll be terribly embarrassed.

"I never invest my money without knowing exactly what I'm buying and who I'm doing business with. I need you to develop this idea more. I'll tell you about my vetting process if we move forward," he tells me.

"I don't want to leave without a yes."

"You don't get a yes on the first appointment. You get a maybe, if you're lucky you get vetted by me."

"It's technically our second appointment. I'm feeling lucky."

He releases a pleasant, low laugh that rumbles up his chest.

"Christos, you just said you want to help me. Do you like my idea?"

"No, I didn't say that. I'm open to the idea, but what I like is your fiery passion for it." He lifts his brows meaningfully.

His grin is irresistibly devastating, and I find myself grinning back.

Something crackles in the air as our gazes hold—something electric and warm, something that comes with knowing someone as more than a stranger. A friend even. A once, long ago, possible *love interest.*

"I'll work on my pitch to give it some clarity," I say.

His eyes roam over my face until they lock back on mine, neither of us smiling anymore. "Good. Call my office when you're ready."

He steps out, and I see that his blonde is waiting for him outside. My heart skids to a stop. Christos doesn't miss my reaction. His eyes shadow speculatively, then he gives me a ghost of a smile and a brief nod, slings his bag behind his shoulder, and walks away.

I smile at his girlfriend. She glares. My smile wavers and I look away, too tempted to look back at him but forcing myself to stare ahead and focus on business.

On the train to Nolita, I try to find the perfect song to reflect how angry I am at myself for fucking up my meeting. And also for feeling...well, the pang I felt when he left for his couples workout with his girl.

I can't deny there's a restless feeling inside me that appears every time I remember he's with her, the same one I felt when she called him darling that first time. It won't go away.

I shut my eyes and try to suppress the memory of his sexy mouth smiling as he cornered me at a party Cole hosted years ago. *"You look like a guy who thinks he's going to kiss me," I teased him. I always teased him with that line. My heart was banging so hard I couldn't think or hardly see straight as he approached...*

But he never got his chance. I never let him, always stealing away when we were alone because he made me nervous.

I sensed he was dangerous to me. I sense he still is.

So I should be glad he's taken. In fact, I'm glad he's taken. It'll totally ensure I always stay focused on business.

yours

Christos
8 1/2 years ago...

"She's yours, Aaric."

For a moment I'm not sure I heard right. Leilani gazes at me with sweet eyes and a smile before glancing down at her very large, very pregnant belly. I blink as I look up at her, struck with disbelief.

I fucked her. Once. And I definitely remember using a rubber.

She glances around. "May I come in? I've been on the road for days. It's been a hassle to find you."

I should be angry. I should demand explanations. It's true I've fantasized about being a father, but she was never the mother I imagined for my child. God, the timing couldn't be shittier. I'm barely getting my fucking feet wet in business. Real business. And I'm in the middle of fucking relocating to New York.

"Ley. I don't have plans for a kid now. I want one. Hell, I want a family more than anything. But not *now*," I say, raking a hand through my hair in exasperation.

She shrugs. "Well, I didn't get pregnant on my own, Christos."

"Jesus," I curse even as I swing the door open and watch her walk inside.

no kidding

Bryn

"It usually only takes two or three meetings, by the third he gives you a yes, a contract is drawn, and you get your first check," Jensen tells me.

I was passing by his Gramercy Park basement flat while walking Missy on Saturday afternoon and decided to punch in his number on my cell and ask if he wanted to meet me outside.

He did.

He's in sweatpants and a sweatshirt, walking next to me after picking up coffee at Irving Place as we head to Washington Square Park.

I mull over his words for a moment and sip the last of my coffee, before tossing it into a nearby trashcan. "This'll be my third meeting and still nothing. I don't know what the fuck is going on—all my meetings have sort of gone south, Sen," I admit.

"Hell, I don't know what to tell you." He scrapes his hand down his jaw and eyes me. "He's breaking protocol seeing you directly. Usually his staff screens possible options first."

"I'd heard that. It's why I was never put through." I hug him with one arm to keep from pulling Missy, Mrs. Lopez's pampered poodle, back. "Thank you, Jensen."

"Hell, don't thank me. I was as surprised he agreed to give you that first meeting as you were. But we had to try, didn't we?"

"Yes, we did." I lean down and pet Missy happily, once again running my plan through my head.

"So when was your last meet?"

"Five days ago? Monday. I was supposed to call but I want to be sure my business plan is solid before I call again. I can't screw this up again."

"I like what you've told me so far."

"Hmm," I say when I spot a man exiting a bank building.

"What the fuck is wrong with you? He said to call, right? You've finally got your foot in the door and now you're hesitating. Why?"

I give him a wordless look, my heart pounding over the reason. "Personal, I guess."

"What."

"I'm attracted to him," I admit, my eyes still tracking the guy, who has his head down and is speaking on the phone.

"So. Last I heard, everyone is. Me included." He grins. "The only ones spared are straight men, and the woman who gave birth to him."

I laugh. "I'm just so impressed by him, Jensen. He was always hardworking, and a little bit bad, but he was a good guy too. I see him, I see the Aaric I knew in this man, but he's also so…I don't know. I'm just impressed by him."

"And."

"And I think, despite him not going for my business, he was impressed too." I smile.

"So?"

"It could just be complicated to work with him so closely, but I'm going to call, don't worry. I'm just getting my ducks in a row."

"Speak of the devil and he appears," he mumbles under his breath, kissing my jaw. "He's crossing the street and heading straight toward you. Go get it."

"Wha—" I gasp, grabbing his wrist impulsively. "Jensen, don't go," I beg.

"I really have to bail, I've got to join my boyfriend in his art stand down Prince Street, it's Saturday, babe! But don't be shy. Pretend he's me and tell him exactly what you told me about your plans for your fucking kickass business. If he's not in, I'll mortgage my house and my ass and give you the money."

"Come on." I push him, laughing, and he pats my butt and says, "Christos," in greeting.

They slap each other's back, and yet I notice Christos seems pissy as he greets him.

I don't know why.

He sees me and I can't stop my heart from kicking faster. "Twice in two weekends?" He smiles, his eyes glinting in the evening light. "Somebody up there has a sense of humor."

"No kidding," I agree.

He's wearing slacks and a gabardine, and he looks decadent. Making it even harder for me to stay calm.

We begin walking side by side toward Washington Square.

"You didn't call," he says. He eyes me sideways.

"I will. I just have other things on my mind. My roommate was really distraught last weekend. I've been looking for more clients so that she can join my dog-walking escapades."

I realize what I said sounds lame. I don't want him to think I let other things keep me from doing what I really want to, so I add, "And I've been quoting an office space, a marketing budget, the works."

"Good. I was concerned I'd discouraged you."

"You have a lot of experience. People with experience have been discouraging me for a while." I shrug.

"Who are these people?"

"Losers, all of them. Just richer."

"'Fess up. Names. Addresses," Christos says.

"Oh haha." I smile. "The loaning institutions."

He frowns, then he leads us into a small café and summons a waitress, giving her a warm smile. "Hi, there. Would you hold this little pooch for us, please? Thank you."

She seems flustered by him, for the waitress nods dumbly and takes the leash from my hand without a glance in my direction—her eyes never leaving Aaric's face.

He sits down at a small table and kicks the chair out so that I can sit with him.

"I'm supposed to be walking Missy, not talking to you," I object.

He winks at the waitress. "Would you walk her up and down the block for a few minutes?" He hands her a bill. "I'll double that if you bring her back safe and happy in fifteen minutes."

"Aaric." I'm amazed, shaking my head. "I think you're having trouble realizing this"—I motion—"is not your office. You're not her boss, mine, or the dog's, or the dog's owner." He leans back and looks at me with smirking eyes.

"You can't just do what you want and get away with it!" I say.

"See...if you want to own your own business...those invisible lines you want to keep yourself inside?" He moves his head sideways decisively. "Need to disappear. No limits to anything you can do. Or have."

I smile as we order drinks. I order more coffee, hoping to keep working tonight, but he orders wine.

"So why did you look me up?" he asks, watching me across the table.

"Bankers don't go into this sort of thing." I shake my head. "Not big risks and definitely not from someone with hardly any credit to her name."

"You're right."

"You think I'm crazy?" I ask.

He just stares at me, his watchful gaze making me nervous.

"A lot of people have thought of crazier stuff that works," I say.

"You can make anything work in this day and age with hard work and a good marketing campaign. I don't think you're crazy. I think you're crazy if you don't call me tomorrow. Do you have any idea how difficult it is to get me to hear anything?" His brows go up cockily.

"I do."

"I've got a full schedule for weeks. If you stop by 6:30 we can discuss some more," he says then.

My stomach dips in excitement and dread. "Okay. Yes. 6:30 p.m. on Monday."

I purse down on my smile and bite it from the inside, trying not to let my nerves and joy show too much.

"Can't believe you still do that," he mutters.

"What?"

"Bite down on your lips like that—from the inside. Beneath your top lip."

I release my lips. "I don't do that," I counter.

"You just did."

"I didn't."

He signals with his index finger. "You just did again."

"Ugh! I'm so annoying," I cry, laughing.

He chuckles. "You're adorable," he says plainly.

We are laughing one second—and the next we are sober.

"So you've been with her for long?"

"Miranda?" he asks. "Six months, give or take."

"A record for you?"

He shrugs. "You could say that."

"Soul mates?"

"I don't believe in that."

"Really?"

"Come on. I'm practical." He frowns. "Do I look like someone who gets caught up in the fanciful stuff?"

I shrug.

"I'm thirty-two, bit."

"So? One can be romantic at any age." I laugh when he doesn't even smile in agreement. God, this man is gorgeous. Gorgeous and very hard to read. "My best friend Becka and I discovered a site called the Soul Mate Site. I love reading it. It preaches that you won't meet your soul mate until you're on your soul's path—so we all better do what we came here to do."

"What did you come here to do?" he asks. He sounds interested.

"I suppose what makes us happy is a good indicator."

"Sometimes it's what we're good at," he says.

I laugh. "Yeah. Maybe. But then you're not thinking you're with your soul mate. You might not be on the right path yet."

"It's the only path I'm going to be on."

I smile. "I heard about you when you made your first million. I was happy for you. You deserve it. While everyone partied you worked, but when you got to the parties you partied hard."

He leans back and crosses his hands behind his head. "I like going all out on everything," he says cockily.

"So are you going all out with your girlfriend?"

He drops his arms. "We'll see," he says. Gruff.

He scrapes his jaw as he stares at a spot past my shoulder in frustration. I realize it's little Missy coming back from her walk.

"I better go. I should probably go to bed early, catch some rest," I say. "You too. I mean. Not together. Alone."

"I know what you mean," he says, taking care of the tab and handing a bill to the waitress.

We head out of the café. I lead Missy to the sidewalk where I see his car is pulling over.

It's a cool night. I feel like curling into him for warmth. My nose feels red, and it's only fall. Christos looks tall and powerful and so warm that it is a feat not to throw myself at him.

"See you Monday," I say.

"Does Missy want a ride?" he asks.

"Oh no, she's good," I say.

"How about Wicked Miss Kelly."

I laugh, blushing so hard the cold fades away.

"Hop in, I'll drop you off," he says.

"I'm fine, thanks. Really," I insist. "Let's keep it professional."

His eyebrows pull down, and he takes a step, looking down at me in a mix of confusion, frustration, and amusement. "I offered you a ride, Bryn. Not a hotel room."

I laugh. "I'm sorry, it's just…" I take a step back and trip over a break in the sidewalk. "I'm within walking distance."

He frowns and steps forward, putting his hand over my waist to keep me from falling. His hand feels so warm I suck up the warmth like a junkie. "You really frustrate me sometimes," he confesses. "You always have."

"What do you mean? Always?"

He smiles, and his hand remains on me for a heart-pounding second. He gradually pulls it free, and I walk away as reluctantly as he removed his hand.

start

Christos

9 years ago...

"So what's her name? The girl back home?"

"Bryn."

"She's nice?"

"She's a little thing."

Leilani puts my hands on her tits and presses them to my chest. "I'm nice too. I can be nice to you."

She wants my dick.

But here I am, months after leaving Austin, still thinking of Bryn Kelly.

"I'm sure she's with some guy now. It should've been me." I get pissed thinking about it. About having to leave to become...well, better. At least *good enough.*

"There's no should've. You're here with me now, and I really want a piece of this gorgeous mouth. I want to feel this big nose...between my thighs."

She squishes closer, and she feels good—warm, giving, her mouth moist as she presses it to mine.

"See, you might pretend I'm her—the first few times— but then you'll forget her. Princess Bryn can go fuck herself."

I let go, incensed. "Never, ever talk about her like that."

"Christos! Come on, please. Christos!!"

Been breaking my back, day in and day out. Sweat and tears…well, sweat and blood, to be more exact.

"What the devil is this?" I laugh at Oswald during our sandwich break under the sparse shade in the construction site. He has a contraption on his ears that he never lets go of.

"I call it the headphone cave."

"What is it for?" I grab it and examine the design. It's awkward and not quite pleasant to the eye, but clearly Oswald likes something about it. "Seems to be a soundproof headset?" I say before I put it on, and all the noise from the construction turns off. Impressed, I pull them off and study them again. "It's pretty genius."

"Right? If only someone could see it."

Someone. I look at him, the word resonating. I shoot him a daredevil look. "Let's play around with it. Make it smaller, more visibly palatable."

"Christ, man."

"What? You don't think we can mass produce and sell this?"

"No. I don't. I don't know shit about that."

"All right. Give me this for a week. You own it. I market it. But we split the profits in half."

"Half of nothing." He chuckles.

"We'll see." Scowling, I toss my can in the trashcan and store the rest of my food away. "You think the guys who made Coca-Cola would've gone anywhere with black water? They fed us all the crap about happiness, life, and good times, sold it and now they're intertwined. Public will buy anything if it's well marketed."

From my old Chevelle, I grab my pen and paper and start to sketch on top of the hood, tearing page after page. "We'll make some stickers, contacting local retailers. It'll take off."

"Come on, I've got a woman and two kids, I can't push something like this."

"I can," I tell him.

I've got nothing holding me back. Just myself. On one side, who I think I am, who I think I deserve to be. On the other, who I know I am, and who I want to be.

I think of Bryn—push the thought away. I cannot do this for her, not even for her. I need to do this for me.

monday

Bryn

I spot a group of homeless people on my way to Christos and Co. on Monday. One of the women among the small group and I make eye contact. She's hauling a cart with recycling cans, her hair is a mess, but her eyes are bright with anticipation when she spots me and asks me for money.

"Sorry, I can't now. But if this goes well, I'll invite you to a meal." I pat my briefcase with all my folders.

"Good luck." She grins.

I head inside, and I meet Aaric at his office again, this time a bit more prepared. This time, I steer clear of the ladies' to avoid any distractions.

With a belly full of nerves and clammy hands, I show him my business plan.

Christos reviews it for ten minutes then nods and hands it back.

He levels me a look that makes my heart skip. How the hell did a boy with an interesting face become the guy with the hottest face in the world?

I wait for him to speak.

And wait and wait.

Until…

"Think bigger. The only way to make money is to take on a certain amount of risk. The higher the risk, the higher the reward," Christos says.

"But it's your money I'm risking."

He nods, very slowly, and then equally slowly—nerve-wrackingly—he stands. He walks over, tips my chin. And tells me, trapping my gaze with his, "Don't worry about the money. I don't care if I lose it. I have plenty. Think bigger, Bryn."

A ghost of a smile touches his mouth as he holds my gaze, and I nod dumbly like that waitress, shaking in my shoes because of his smile. It's gone all too soon, and he drops his hand, back to business, and heads to his desk.

"Expand your concept. I'd be giving you the biggest safety net you could ever have in investing. I'm telling you it's okay if you lose all my money. I want you to think big."

"This *is* big," I mumble, absently brushing my hand across the lingering tingles on my chin. "This is all I want to do, Aaric."

I hate that I sound defeated and pleading, but I'm at a loss as to what else to say at this point.

He leans forward, his tone of voice almost intimate. Low. "See, bit, that's the thing. The world doesn't care how you personally feel about what you're doing. You can hate it, and be good at it, and that's all that matters to them. So in order for us to get you doing what you want to do, you need to give your potential customers what they want. Even, what they don't know they want…because no one has given it to them yet."

"But *I*…will?" I say, reading his train of thought and feeling inspired by it.

His lips curl in quiet male pride.

I gather my things and silently walk away. Hating how hard my heart is pounding—not because of his momentary rejection, but because of HIM.

The way it felt to have his thumb and forefinger on my chin.

The way I wanted the rest of his hand on my face, for everything to miraculously go poof and go away, including the briefcase I'd had on my lap, and for the warmth of his body to be flush against mine. Or rather, mine against his.

Crazy that Aaric only embraced me once when we were kids, but my body cannot seem to forget (and admittedly and uncomfortably, *long* for a repeat). Even when he was skinnier, he was warm and comforting.

Yet also a little bit too exciting.

"What the fuck, he said it's okay to lose his money? He *never* does that. He's always threatening and he never makes investments he knows he will lose—he always knows he'll win back something," Jensen says, confused.

I shrug and tug Natchez toward the park, feeling a bit discouraged after days of thinking and being unable to amp up my proposal.

Why would Christos risk his neck for me? My business plan is a piece of shit. My whole damn life is shit. I've had three meetings with Christos and still nothing.

Here I am in New York, a city I'd still get lost in if I wandered out far enough, with a project I've had years to plan and is still no closer to maturing, and lusting after another woman's man, unable to make my project even remotely interesting to him.

"Why can't I be like you, Natchez?" I ask the Husky, stroking the flat of his back as he turns his head and licks my bare calf. "Oh, you think it's all solved with a lick. That's not real life, buddo. At least that's not real life for *humans*. Hmm? But give me another one?" I let him sniff my hand, and he licks my fingers, and I giggle happily.

That evening, I sit with my computer, my drawings, my plan. And ask myself repeatedly the same questions he's asked me.

What will differentiate my business from them?

What can I offer the market that is fresh and different?

God. I look at all of his success and I can't even get on my feet on my own.

But I'm doing this.

I spend all weekend cooped up, trying to make sense of this dream of mine. I think of my parents—what I learned from them.

I remember opening Kelly's. I remember how I used to be asked questions all the time from customers. Does this shirt match this skirt?

"You're a visual person. You see things that aren't there," my mother would tell me. Aunt Cecile would gush about the simple but pretty outfits I always wore. Could I incorporate it into the business?

By next Monday, I decide not to call Christos and Co. but head over there instead.

Once again, the homeless woman asks me for money.

"*Soon.* Wish me luck," I promise, giving her an apple I brought for her instead.

"Good luck," she says distractedly, gazing down at the apple.

I wait patiently outside his office for his appointment to leave—and when Christos appears at the door, I rise to my feet.

Our eyes lock—and hold.

"I want to meet up with you," I say.

He raises one eyebrow at me, then two. Shooting a chiding glance at his assistant, she starts to apologize, "She refused to—"

He quiets her by making a "five minute" sign, and then he nods me into his office. "You know you're the first person who just walks in here expecting to be seen because she feels like it?"

"Well, it's important." I walk forward and take a seat across from his desk as he takes his.

"First of all, I need to ask: why are you helping me?"

He shoots me a look. "I'm not helping you yet."

"I think you are. You're being more than generous with your time and patience," I say.

There's a moment of quiet as we stare at each other. Christos then leans back, scraping his thumb along his lower lip as he looks at me. "You're responsible, you're honest, you take criticism well, you don't retreat in your shell and cry about it. You go and fix what needs to be fixed, you have vision, and that's what makes a great entrepreneur."

God, I think my heart just skipped a thousand times, one for each word. "Do you mean that?" I ask.

"Do you have to ask that?"

The look he sends me clearly states he's a man who means what he says...

I exhale and shoot him a look of gratitude.

"Okay. So I've got a great idea," I tell him as I pull out my presentation. "I've even hashed out a business plan. Aside from our head department store in New York, and a kickass website—both carrying exclusive items that I will design along with the top-selling women's fashion brands—House of Sass will be a personalized, trendy, fashion-stylist software. I have here some studies that prove that women dressed the part make better decisions and act more confidently and get more done when they're confident about their looks. I want to offer them an app that will act as their personal stylist, with a push of a button. May I?"

I motion to approach, and Christos—hot in slacks and a white shirt—is watching me with a sparkle in his eye as he nods.

I take my phone and show him the small test application that I tried out with a developer this week.

"It's not done yet, but you have the best tech people around," I explain, blushing when I realize this must look so rustic to him. "This is homemade. I'm hoping with your loan..." I turn to meet his gaze, and look away when I realize he's very, very close, "the software can be fully developed. Its database can include location and weather...top-selling products from around a certain mile range nearby...suggestions on what's in style if you choose to amp up your spring, fall, winter, and summer wardrobes with a few must-have pieces. If the trends are thick belts, chunky bead necklaces, whatever's up. "It's like a personal shopper and closet organizer in one. And it can be accessible to everyone, even people with no budget. All it would require of them is less than a day to input their closet pieces. Picture upload (keywords) and the software does the rest. It'll save you so much time in the long run."

I click on a button that reads "Night out."

And a list of three options appears.

"See, these are actual pieces that I own," I say, feeling his gaze over my shoulder as he studies it.

"It's suggesting sweaters and leggings, boots, and wide belts, because that's a current trend. And it's supposed to be cool tonight. Now...if we want to make this edgier, we can have users interact with one another. I can give my friend access to my closet to either borrow pieces or vote on my suggested outfits for my occasions."

"Not a bad idea," he murmurs. Impressed.

"It's amazing what the right clothes can do for a woman," I say, stepping back.

"Did it pick that out for you?" He motions to my black leggings and long sweater.

"No," I admit. "I sold my wardrobe. To pay a software developer to help me chalk this up. But I kept some key pieces, mostly black or white, which I can mix and match. And my best pair of flats, stilettos, and boots." I smile. "You realize you don't need more if they're well chosen."

"One problem," he frowns as he props back against his desk, folding his arms, "is the time it takes to input a closet."

"I thought of that. But if we had representatives in every state, we could charge a small fee, like ninety-nine dollars, for one of our reps to go to your home and spend an afternoon inventorying your closet."

For the next half hour, we discuss my expanded ideas on the store, and I tell him why I think it can be special, how targeting trendy women of all ages would be ideal.

He seems vaguely interested, until his assistant rings him up to tell him his next appointment has arrived.

"This meeting is adjourned."

I quickly gather my things, hating that time flew by so fast. "So it's a yes? Say it's a yes, Christos. You want to say it. I know it," I bluff.

"Work on it."

His grin is so irresistible, I'm grinning too. "Can I wait for you outside to talk some more?"

"Don't think so. I'm heading to the gym at 6." He dials to his assistant. "Show him in."

I force myself to leave, checking to see how much time I need to kill before it's 6 p.m.

I spend the next hour walking Brooklyn, thinking of ideas as I wait for it to be six p.m. and corner him on his way to the gym.

My dad used to tell me the best thing he could ever give me was an education. I didn't waste what I could get. Even when they died in the fire at the Las Vegas hotel and I quit college shortly after, I always tried using what education I *did* get. I went to live with my aunt Cecile, and kept thinking that I would do something with this education my parents had given me.

My first business, at eight, was a lemonade stand. It flopped. Nobody walked down the cul-de-sac where we lived—I had like one customer, total (my mom.) Even then, I always wanted to do something with my time. Something lasting. I wanted security and I knew, after losing my parents, only I could provide it to myself. I tried my hand at everything. But plants died. Even my goldfish died. Still, it didn't keep me from wanting to put myself out there, create things, do things.

I promised my aunt Cecile that I'd be sure we were comfortable at all times in our lives. Even old age. I was thinking ahead. Unfortunately, my determination didn't prepare me for failure times a dozen.

I always picked myself straight up by my bootstraps and kept going, though, certain that the wheel of fortune would keep turning and one day, I'd succeed.

It wasn't until after the store closed, after Mom and Dad passed, that I realized I'd had a natural talent for dressing the mannequins, and later, for mending and revamping my own clothes.

And it wasn't until after many bad jobs, and a shit-ton of tears, that I realized I wasn't only good at it, I enjoyed it. And it wasn't until my aunt Cecile died that I realized…I was in my mid-twenties, a college dropout (I'd had to drop out to take care of my aunt), and should definitely think about doing something about my situation before I turned thirty.

I'm thirty now—and I have no more minutes to spare.

So, at 6 p.m., waiting for my future business partner and investor outside the Christos and Co. building, I rehearse the rest of what else I'm going to say. My pitch, as they say.

Some tag line, some brilliant marketing idea, something the man will find irresistible.

He exits and immediately spots me outside, not once breaking his stride.

"I didn't realize I'd have an escort." He removes his jacket and slings his duffel behind his shoulders.

"You're amusing yourself with me, but that's not a problem if you give me twenty more minutes to discuss my project," I say.

His lips begin tugging at the corners then. "I'll give you an hour if you keep doing a good job amusing me."

"Goodness," I exaggerate. "Are you that hard to keep entertained?"

"Hard to please."

"And I'm pleasing you?"

"Pretty close to that."

"Hmm." I bite down on my lip under my top lip, then I notice he's staring at me. At my mouth.

I let go and exhale, then I jump into the rest of my presentation.

We walk past the woman who asked me for money on my way in, the one I promised to invite to dinner if all went well.

As I explain to Christos why I think this is the best business, best timing, everything, she approaches.

"Did it go well?" she asks, eyes wide with hope.

"Oh, I'm not sure yet." I glance at my future business partner. "Say yes so I can take her out to dinner," I order.

"No," he says sternly, slipping her a bill. "Go to dinner on your own, she's busy."

I hope he means to talk to me when he suddenly makes a right turn and disappears into a gym. *Ooops.* I have to backtrack when I realize I was heading in the wrong direction.

I hurry into the gym after him. He signs in and gives me a stern sideways look, but then he motions me in with a jerk of his chin and scribbles down his signature again. Silently, I walk behind him as he heads into an area of private saunas.

He walks into the changing room, and I almost walk into the door.

I wait nervously outside, then I see him step out in nothing but a tiny towel and a shit ton of muscles, ignoring me as he heads into a large private sauna. I hesitate for a second, then forge ahead and pry the door open, peering in through the smoke.

I hear his voice from the far end. He seems to be the only one here. "If you plan to be here, go change."

Nodding even though he might not be able to see me through the mist, I head into the women's changing room.

I undress quickly, wrap a towel around myself, and head back into his sauna.

I walk inside as the door shuts behind me, sealing us in heat and steam. I'm so nervous that I continuously ensure that I'm firmly wrapped in the white towel.

"You're quite a little bulldozer, aren't you, Bryn?"

Christos sits on a bench at the far end. His hips still wrapped in a white towel. His eyes gleaming in the misty shadows.

He sounds amused and, though his words are playful, I can see a spark of respect in his gaze. Smoke fills the cabin as I find a place to sit across from his large, barely clad body.

My eyes fall on a large figure shaped by his towel and, with a kick of my heart, I realize what it is.

His cock imprint.

Breathless in an instant, I glance away because that's not really my business. His cock is not my business. The fact that it is so noticeable and large?

Not my business.

Not my problem.

"I do my best thinking sweating," he says, leaning back and planting his arms at his sides and *Bryn, really! Stop gaping at his tattoo.*

I retrieve my gaze as quickly as possible and gaze at the floor. But it's such a lovely tattoo. Running up his shoulder, spreading out into a part of his pec.

I pat the sweat on my face with a small towel, already breathing hard but trying not to be too obvious.

"I find that very inconvenient," I huff, patting my face with the small towel again. The towel around my chest sort of loosens a fraction with the movement—and his eyes fall there.

And stay there.

Right on the edge of my towel, where my cleavage is.

His voice is the opposite of silky, rough and low. "Your towel's on the edge."

I'm mesmerized by the change in his voice.

And the heavy, lazy-sexy look in his eyes.

"On the edge of what?"

His lips curve. So devilishly my heart skids. He reaches out to tuck the towel back in, his index finger brushing against the top swell of my breast as he does.

I gulp. Hard.

Aaric withdraws his finger.

The air is hot inside the sauna, but no part of my body feels as *hot* as the part of skin he just touched.

"Thank you," I breathe as I nervously retuck the towel.

He grins, crosses his arms behind his head. "You're welcome."

I exhale, not even knowing where to put my eyes, trying to ignore his magnetic pull. The way the sweat starts to glisten on his chest, coating his tanned skin and muscles.

The steam keeps coming, and Aaric just looks at me.

He just looks at me.

"I knew you were different, when we were kids," I don't know why I admit, but I feel like maybe if I put this out there, the tension I feel when I'm around him will ease. This will put us in friendly mode, and I need friendly mode with him. "You made me feel different. I had to be careful with you. But even with the guys that I dated that seemed more harmless, it was bad news in the end. The good times aren't even really that good. I didn't want that to happen with you too."

He frowns then, leaning forward, his expression unreadable but at the same time, his eyes sharp with interest. "Any particular reason they weren't worth it?"

"Because the guys don't get me. It's like every time I blurt out the wrong thing I want to shove something into my mouth. I feel mortified when I see them get embarrassed. I feel odd and like I just don't fit. I just don't fit as the second part of a relationship, I'm just too guarded. Maybe I'm too independent. My friendship with you was more important to me, I realized. At the time."

More silence.

More nerve-wracking green-gold stare. "Is there a reason you're telling me this?"

"Yes. I wanted you to know why I never wanted to go there with you. I was scared that you were too valuable to me."

I fall silent, and Aaric says nothing, and there's still so much I want to say that I can't seem to find the way to as he keeps waiting...for me to say more. There's all this tension in my body—the opposite of what I thought would happen happened. Our naked bodies are sweating underneath two mere towels.

I'm fully aware of every inch of this man, of every inch of my own body and what his nearness does to me.

I want to steal my hands under his.

Climb them up his muscled thighs, and touch him, and make him hard for me as I kiss and caress him. Make him want me like he once did.

Make him try again because this time I won't even hesitate, I'd go for it—recklessly and without restraint because I never want to go to bed with my what if to dream up a thousand kisses from him that never came because I said no. So one kiss has turned into a thousand, and the way I wanted him has multiplied by those thousand kisses, and none of them are real, but they're real enough to haunt me, to make me want it, to make me wonder how he would kiss me.

If he'd have been gentle and sweet to me, or rough and a little crude and dirty, or maybe some way I couldn't have even imagined.

"So did you let me in here to listen to more of my plan, or are you planning to discourage me from wanting to do business with you?"

"I let you in here for reasons I can't even comprehend." He shoots me a vexed look, his expression bleak and dire.

I laugh, figuring he's playing with me. "I can't lose this chance, Aaric. I really want this. It's easy for you to string me along when you've never lost anything at all."

"I've lost something."

It's not just the words, but the tone he uses that makes me sit up straighter. I'm too surprised to do more than drink in the stormy, shadowed look in his eyes. Shit. I hit a sore spot. Way to go, Bryn. Nice way to endear yourself to him.

"I'm sorry," I say.

"Fuck. I'm sorry too." He scrapes a hand down his face, sweat glistening all across his gorgeous body.

"So what was it? That you lost." Suddenly—belatedly—I remember his mother and I want to slap myself for speaking so abruptly.

"Somebody," he says.

Your mom, I think. "You loved her."

"Aside from my mom," he adds. "Yes, but I never got the chance to love her. She died when she was born."

Shock makes my eyes flare wide open. Whaaat? "You had a daughter?"

He meets my gaze and I see everything I need to see in his eyes.

"And your wife?"

"Not wife. Friend."

"What happened?"

"She got depressed, left my life, fell in love later, got married. We talk occasionally."

"Oh. I'm glad." I glance away, then back at him. "I'm sorry about that."

He nods as he looks at me.

I just stare back at him, suddenly understanding more. My heart is doing weird things in my chest. I want to embrace him. I want to run away from him. I want to open up and talk more about our losses. I want to pretend we've never lost a thing.

I swallow.

He leans back, the move sort of implying he doesn't want to speak more about it.

Patting my face with the towel, my breathing fast as my body keeps on sweating and I keep spewing out feelings as if they're attached to my sweat.

"See, sometimes I'm feeling lonely like nothing will ever turn out my way. I feel different, like a red ink stain on a page full of gold dots."

"I know what you mean. I used to feel like I was a tear on a page, not a red ink stain though."

"Why? Like you tore the page?"

"Yep."

"Like you're the tear on a page?"

"Yep."

"Wow, that's awful. Are you okay?"

"Obviously I'm not."

"Yeah. Sigh." I laugh.

"Go on. You were saying," he prods.

"Oh nothing, only that all these feelings go away when you're close."

Shadows darken his eyes, as if my comment gets to him.

"Why is that." His stare becomes intense enough to singe me to my bones.

"Because another feeling comes in when you're close and it's all I can feel. Like a glass of oil is overflowing with water until the oil overflows and then it's just the most fresh and hydrating water."

"I'm the water in your glass." He starts to smile in bemusement, but his gaze doesn't lose one single bit of its intensity.

I laugh. "You fill my glass. I suppose you're the water too."

He grins even more, like this is the best compliment he's ever gotten.

He leans forward, his gaze level with mine. We're both glistening with droplets of steam and sweat, but his stare is the most heavenly thing I've ever seen look at me. So serious, so sure. "I had no idea," he says, the green in his eyes more vivid than ever, "how much I missed you, bit."

It's so intense I drop my gaze and pull it back to his, my stomach sort of turning in on itself. "Why. Do I fill your glass too?"

"Not sure." He winks, smirking. "Maybe you just fill my well, girl."

I laugh, and he chuckles, and we sort of spend the next minutes in silence, our smiles lingering on our faces.

By the time we leave the sauna, I feel good. Physically, I'm relaxed, but emotionally, I'm in a bit of chaos/confused mode. Christos offers to drive me home, but I decline. An hour later, a message appears on my phone.

Tomorrow. Next appointment. 8 p.m. @ Peasant (Nolita). Be there.

I'm *so* there.

Midnight text to BFF:

Do you remember when you stole into the guys' locker room to chase after Lyle?

Becka: No. I promptly forgot that when the coach found me before Lyle did and called my parents about what a perv I was.

Me: Okay, forget that part. Imagine that you'd found Lyle. In nothing but this tiny towel. Like a fig leaf, that small.

Becka: Okay, what's going on?

Me: It's Christo's fault. We went to a sauna and...we went to a sauna.

Becka: And? Dish out!!!

Me: And...muscular man. Tiny towel! Heat and sweat? Ugh. I'm still squirming inside.

Becka: Baby girl, that's hot! I vote you go impale yourself on Christos. I sure as hell remember he'd like that.

Me: Not anymore. He's taken, okay.
Lucky bitch ☹

Becka: All is fair in love and war.

Me: It's not love.

Becka: What is it?

Me: Terrible
Terrible lust

Becka: Was he really muscled? He was skinny before. No?

Me: You have NO idea the muscles he packs. And I won't even get into the SHAPE of what was under his towel.

Becka: Now who's the perv! HA!

Me: Lucky I don't have a principal after me. (But maybe an angry girlfriend if she ever found out her man was with me in a sauna? I'd be jealous out of my mind!)

Becka: Me thinks you're in trouble, bestie... ☺ ☺ ☺

Me: Nooooo. I just needed that off my chest. I'm good now. I'm going to work!!

Really.

No, really.

Not thinking of Christos's sweaty, tattooed bod in a tiny towel at all! ☺

I dreamed of him. He was hugging me in his office, and I was crying on his shoulder because my parents had just died. It makes no sense. He wasn't there when my parents died, flowers sent in his absence. The only time he ever hugged me was when we said goodbye. And maybe...well, it wasn't exactly a hug, but when he tried to kiss me. Still, he didn't hug me in his office yesterday. But when I wake in the middle of the night, my face is wet and I can't go back to sleep.

It feels odd to see him, remember the girl I used to be—he reminds me of my childhood. He reminds me of my dreams, my parents, myself before my heart broke into pieces, one for each person I've loved and lost.

Maybe, even, including him.

I'm distracted with Milly, Natchez, and the rest of my dog tribe the next day. Then Milly's owner, Mrs. Ford, invites me to join her for tea when I drop Milly off that afternoon.

"Brynny! You're back just in time for tea. Come sit with Milly and me."

"Oh, Mrs. Ford...I couldn't..."

"You can and you will," she declares in moody New York fashion.

So I grudgingly agree, "Five minutes," and sit in her European-style sitting room, drinking tea.

"Tell me about yourself, Brynny. How are you finding New York?"

"I'm finding it," I say, and she laughs. I admit, "It's a jungle, Mrs. Ford, but I suppose I'm learning the ropes of how to survive around here."

"Like what?"

"Like if I stand at the pizza line and don't know exactly, *exactly*, what I'm having when it's my *turn*, I get *skipped*."

We laugh, and she tells me of the days when she moved into Manhattan seven years ago.

"At my age, you can imagine what a shock the city was. It's why I'd rather look at the city from up here." She motions to her lovely view, and I say, "If you ever want to go out, I'd be happy to walk with you or ride with you anywhere."

"Thank you, but I do have family who visits occasionally. But thank you for offering, Brynny."

I feel relieved that she's not alone in the city—mainly because I don't know what I would have done if I hadn't met Sara when I got here—so I smile, make her a new pot of tea, and head out, not before petting Milly. "'Bye, girl," I whisper in her ear. "Wish me luck tonight."

I rush to get ready for my meeting, more nervous than I care to admit.

'bye, bit

Christos
12 years ago

She finds me out on the roof while the party disperses inside. I'm staring at the lake in the distance, an empty bottle in my hand.

Bryn walks forward, her steps tentative. It's as if she thinks I'll ask her to leave. No. I'd never ask her to leave. I crave her too much to want her anywhere but near me.

"Are you out here all alone because you're avoiding saying goodbye to me?" she asks.

Her mouth drives me crazy when she speaks. I try to pull my head on straight and shake it. "Nah." I smile.

She frowns at me. She's always told me I'm very elusive and stubborn, the one man she can never read. "I'll leave. Really. If you don't want me here."

"Don't leave. Come here, bit." I scoot over.

"Bit?"

"You're a small little thing. Much more trouble than you look."

"I'm not trouble."

"The places you take a guy's thoughts...pure trouble, bit."

She smiles happily, and takes a seat next to me, and thanks to the wind, her hair flies across my face. I brush it back, trying not to snatch it between my fingers. "You going to miss anything about here?" she asks me.

"I'm going to miss you." I smile. "Hey, you sad?"

Her eyes shadow, but she shakes it off. "What? You think I'd miss you?" she scoffs.

I nod soberly. "I'd take you with me if I could."

"I wouldn't go." She wrinkles her nose.

"You would if I asked you to." I smile, and she laughs, then we fall silent.

"I guess this is the last time I see you, huh," she says.

I look at her closely. If anything in this goddamned world would prompt me to stay here—it's her. But there's a job for me in Dallas, an opportunity for me to grow. "Don't change, bit."

"I'll try. And you. Be good, Aaric. The line you walk is far too fine."

I laugh. She glances at the skyline, as if realizing it's too late. People have already left the party.

"Have a good life," she says, clapping her hands once. As if that's that.

I frown. "Jesus. I might see you one day."

"Really? I'm not sure you will."

"I might look you up one damn day."

"Why?"

"To prove to you that I can. To show you how far I'm going to have come."

"You'll want to show off what a big shot you are."

"That's right." I wink. "Bye, bit."

Her eyes water and when I rise to my feet and draw her into my arms—for the first and last time, really—she sobs into my shoulder and can't seem to say it back.

1 a.m.

Bryn

I meet him at Peasant as instructed, my pulse a little rapid as I walk inside, even with the two glasses of wine I guzzled down to help with the nerves as I changed. It's as if my nervousness keep amping up with every meeting. I don't know if it's because I'm nervous that one final NO, and this will be over. Or if it's because I really crave to spend time with him and look forward to these...meetings. Stressful as they are.

Anyway, I wanted this to go well. So I pulled out the mini-dress Sara calls the "tiny sexual bomb" that I designed myself, and I headed several blocks from our apartment down to Peasant.

My heart does something crazy when my eyes spot Christos at the bar. His head is bent to his phone, and he's frowning over something he's reading.

He's wearing a black shirt and gray slacks, his hair slicked back, and he looks drool-worthy. I lick my lips, and then he tilts his head as if he senses me, and my heart flips a little more.

Please like this little dress, I pray as I draw in a breath and wind toward the bar.

Then I wonder why I want him to like it—if for my business, or for me—and I annoy myself for wondering when the answer isn't clear.

He's on his feet, and I can't say he's smiling with that full mouth of his, but his eyes are definitely smiling at me.

He smells like cologne and freshly used soap, and warm skin. "This is a House of Sass dress," I say, in greeting, when I stop so close to him his delicious scent is in every nook and cranny of my lungs.

"I like it," he says, his voice sort of moving the hair on the top of my head as he looks down at me, and because my legs don't feel too steady, I take one of the bar stools.

Christos takes his stool, and when a glass of wine appears within my view, I take a long gulp.

"It's not water, bit," I hear Christos rasp amusedly in my ear as he reaches out, taking the glass from me. "You're better off letting it breathe." He twirls it, slow and easy, *letting it breathe*, and I'm the one who can't breathe when my eyes meet his.

He's really close. Much closer than I ever get him in his office.

It's nerve-wracking.

Familiar but new.

Exciting.

I can see flecks inside his eyes, the lightness of the tips of his lashes, and the laugh lines drawn around the corners of his eyes.

"I'm thirsty," I breathe in answer, and he hands it back after looking at my mouth.

Offering him a shy smile, I take another long gulp, the tension between us so palpable it feels as if any word would shatter it like glass.

"Okay, so this is good. I'm getting the money?" I ask him as he only watches me drink from the wine, his eyes holding a mischievous, secret gleam that makes me crave to know what he thinks.

Chuckling softly, he twirls his own glass of wine, and says, "No. We're just getting started. The vetting process is just getting started." He leans forward, his gaze probing and inquisitive. "How much time are you going to dedicate to the business? And how much personal money have you invested so far?"

"I'd dedicate as much time to the business as you'd need. I just need six hours of sleep a day, and I'm willing to invest the 3,450 dollars I've got saved."

He nods at that, shifting his legs under the stool to face me more fully. The move bringing his knee up to bump into the side of my thigh.

I swallow back a little gasp of surprise, but he doesn't seem to notice. "What is your daily schedule like, bit?"

"I, well…"

"Do you sleep?"

"Yes."

"How many hours?"

"Seven. Eight."

He says nothing, sipping his drink. His knee still touching the side of my thigh. "Any routines before bed?" he then asks.

"Um…No. I wear socks, but take them off in the middle of the night." I avoid telling him that I do have a thing for alarm clocks. *Ugh.*

"Why is that?" he says. Referring to my socks.

"I like my feet cold."

He chuckles, shaking his head, and my skin pricks pleasurably at the sound of his chuckle and at the barest shift from his knee against my thigh.

I feel vulnerable—telling him how I sleep. I can't suppress the embarrassment from my voice when I breathe, "Do you vet everyone like this?"

Christos notices I'm flustered, and he calmly explains. "I'm investing in the person, not in the business. The business doesn't exist, currently."

"True."

"I want to know who I'm getting in bed with. So to speak." He shoots me a wily grin, and that wicked smile of his causes my brain to scatter.

"Well, I won't tell you a single other thing until you return the favor. Tell me more about you, Aaric," I say.

He motions the bartender for something, then turns his attention back to me.

"What do you want to know?"

"I don't know. How long have you been living in Manhattan?"

"About nine years."

"Why Manhattan?" I frown curiously.

"I followed the money trail." He winks, then watches as they bring us two glasses of ice water. Christos has already pulled out my updated business plan and is scanning it when they set them before us.

"No ice. She doesn't like ice. Thanks." He hands over my glass to the bartender and starts reading my business plan.

I blink.

"How do you remember that?" I'm mind-blown by the fact that he remembers.

He lifts his brows.

"I didn't like ice in high school; it made my throat hurt," I admit. "But it's always a hassle for people to take it back, so I've gotten used to it and don't return my glasses anymore."

He eyes the bartender and motions at the glass he was setting back. "Take that back and bring the lady one with no ice?"

The bartender scurries away, and I swallow, smiling to myself.

"You always brought tension to the parties," I tease.

"Tension." A smile ruffles his sexy mouth for a brief moment before he somberly replies. "It's not your problem if what you want is a hassle for someone. You take care of yourself or nobody else will." His eyes gleam protectively on my face for a heart-stopping moment.

I bite down on my lip and then realize his eyes fall there. I can't breathe as he stares at my mouth.

"Are you dating anyone?" he asks then. His voice gruff.

My breath catches even more.

"Um. Why?"

He's silent.

"Oh. The vetting. I'm sorry, I…" I shake my head, cursing myself for thinking he was asking for himself. "No. Of course not. I haven't found the right guy." I lower my reddening face, hoping he doesn't realize I'm talking about maybe… well. Him. "Looks like you found your Miss Right." I lift my gaze.

My smile fades; his eyes are intense as he looks at my whole face as if memorizing it all over again.

"We made sense," he says.

"Made?" I'm feeling a little light-headed, so I'm impressed that I catch on to this so fast.

"Make," he coolly corrects.

"I ended up giving my V card to Ted Cross," I blurt.

"Rowdy Ted?" He seems surprised and instantly vexed.

"Yep."

Christos says nothing. I have more wine to try to quell the heat his possessive stare is generating. But it's no use.

His body is so close to mine, all my cells are buzzing.

"I was nervous about the whole process. Look! Don't look at me like that. If I'd wanted someone thorough and good with his hands, I'd have given it to someone like…well, you."

I take a quick breath of utter astonishment when I realize what I'd said.

I'm fully buzzed.

Fully stupid drunk.

Fuck, I need to stop drinking, but instead I take another sip.

All while Christos's gold-green laser-like gaze is locked on me like a missile target. "He was no good for you."

I look down at my lap. "I know. But I didn't want it to mean something. I didn't want to make a fuss of it. I didn't want you to think I was awkward at it. So I gave it to him."

He stares at me, the muscle in his jaw working as he looks at the bar as if trying to get a grip of some unnamable emotion.

"He was no good for you," he repeats. Softer this time. As his eyes slide back to mine.

Intimacy—it's all over. In how close his eyes are looking into mine, how close his leg is to mine, his shoulder, his elbow, to *mine.*

"See? This is what you get for asking so many questions. TMI. And now awkward silence. And a drunk client-slash-business-partner or whatever."

He stops me from drinking more with a hand motion, then signals for the check.

I bite my lip on the inside. "I wasn't ready for you then," I admit.

He winks at me. "Nobody ever is. Come here. Lean on me." He raises me from the chair and I slip my arm around his waist as we head outside, where his car waits.

"I'm only two blocks away," I say as he leads me to his car.

"Then I'll walk you there."

"I'm going to regret all this tomorrow, won't I?"

An irresistible grin appears on his face and it makes my knees wobble even worse. "Nah. I don't think you've stepped far enough beyond your comfort zone to regret a thing."

"My comfort zone is very close to me; I'm already stepping dangerously outside," I contradict.

I lean into him as we head down the block.

I'm acutely aware of the buzzing energy of his body walking next to mine, his arm holding me up by the waist. I want to die a little. He's a powerful, attractive man and I'm only human, and maybe a bit too alchoholized for my liking.

"Say something." My voice is soft. Worried. As I look up at his profile.

"Your smell does shit to me," he gruffs out.

His presence is intense and overwhelming as he stares down at me and then, frowning and thoughtful, at the street ahead.

I laugh, and so does he.

But we're not laughing in the next instant when we reach my building and face each other.

"Say you won't take any of this seriously," I beg.

He nods.

"I mean I hardly know what I'm saying," I explain.

He silences me with his thumb. "Then stop talking," he says gently.

I swallow, then lean on him again.

Christos is quiet. I am too.

He puts his arm around my shoulders, and I press my cheek to his chest as he leads me up my elevator, into my apartment, my room, and then into bed, where I kick my shoes off before he tucks me in. "I'd like a do-over of tonight," I say.

"I can make that happen."

"Thank you." I slip into my bed, then realize I need to set my alarms. "Oh shit."

I rummage through the nightstand drawer.

"Tell me where your socks are and I'll bring them over," he says as he closes my curtains.

"No, it's just that..." I take out my five small alarm clocks, each a different size and shape. "My parents slept through the hotel fire." I set the first one for 1 a.m.

He watches me from the foot of the bed, his brows practically joined over his nose as he tries to make sense of what I'm doing.

"They were on their anniversary trip. Twenty years. They were the only ones that didn't hear the alarm," I explain.

"I got it," he says, crossing over and taking one of the alarm clocks from me.

"So what do you do when they ring?" he asks, flipping them on, one by one.

"Nothing." I sigh, exasperated with myself as I drop my head back on my pillow. "I just make sure everything is calm and quiet. Then I fall instantly asleep."

Watching him turn on the last alarm clock, I rest my head on the pillow again and look at him. His face etched to perfection, creased with puzzlement as he finishes his task.

He smells really good. Like incredibly good.

"Are you mad I didn't tell you? When you asked before?" I'm worried. I can't help it.

He raises his eyes to meet mine.

Is there tenderness there? I feel mushy under his gaze.

"No," he says. "I could tell you were evading. I knew there was more. You going to be okay?" he asks, his voice husky with tenderness as he tips my face up by the chin.

"Hmm. Stay."

I don't know if he will. He heads outside. I hear him make a call. He comes back in, tilts my chin back up.

I like it so much I want to push the rest of my face into his hand. "I can't stay," he says.

"You can't? Or you don't want to?"

"I can't. It's not just your scent. You do shit to me. You understand?" His eyes blaze in the shadows—the heat and intensity roiling in their gold depths making my stomach constrict. "The only thing that can keep me away from you tonight is distance."

I nod, ever so slowly.

"It's not convenient for you, is it?" I ask, breathless.

"No, bit, it's not *convenient*." His smile is devastating as he pulls up my covers. "I thought I finally had my shit together and then you come along to fuck it up. You tend to do that to me—you really are quite the Wicked Miss Kelly."

I grin.

He brushes his thumb over my lips. One second.

The best second of my adult life.

"Good night, bit."

"'Night."

We stare at each other for longer than necessary, then he walks away.

When my alarm sounds at 1 a.m. all I know is all is okay, but it's not, not really, and I don't know why it doesn't feel like it is.

where is she?

Christos

12 1/2 years ago...

I ask Cole where she'll be Saturday—he tells me at Kelly's, so I stop by the department store and find her behind a register, giving instructions to a new employee. She spots me and her honeyed eyes widen in surprise. "I'm taking a small break, but call me if you have any questions." A pop of pink appears on her cheeks as she hurries out from behind the counter and toward the west side of the ground floor.

I follow her down the hall and toward a small office with her mother's name, Katherine Kelly, embossed on it.

She walks inside, grabs a drink from the fridge, and offers me one.

I shake my head and just smile—taking a good look at her. Enjoying how frazzled she seems by my presence.

She takes a huge sip, leaning back on her mother's desk, then she sets the drink aside. "What?" She touches her mouth, as if she thinks she's got something on it.

"What what?" I counter.

"Why are you looking at me like that?"

"How am I looking at you, bit?"

She struggles for a reply, her cheeks very flushed, very fucking adorable. "You look like a boy who thinks he'll get to kiss me."

My eyebrows rise. "I'm not a boy."

She clears her throat, bristling and turning around. "No, but you're kind of a jerk."

I grab her wrist, smiling as I turn her back. "I will kiss you though." At her wide-eyed look, I nod. "Cole told me he told you I like you."

"He did, did he? Cole's been very busy."

"He's an idiot."

She bites down on her laugh. "Then why are we discussing him?"

"Because in this case, lips..."—I lift my hand to grab her by the back of the neck, my other hand coming to her mouth, unable to keep myself from touching the soft, silky flesh—"he's right."

I brush my thumb over that mouth. Sexy little Bryn Kelly. One day, she walked in with her father to the shop where Cole and I worked. I went stone cold. She glanced at me before leaving, and I almost went and searched her pockets to see if she'd taken my brain with her.

I can't think of shit since I met this girl.

She's younger than I am, and shy. From a well-known family. Better than I deserve.

But I want her anyway.

I want to treat her like a princess, wish I could offer her the treasures of a queen. My mother is dying. The only thing keeping Cole and I in Austin is her. This is where she was born. This is where her roots are.

I've hated everything about Austin except

This

Girl

HERE.

"In fact, I think I'll kiss you right now." I continue to purposefully touch the bottom lip she bites.

God, that flush is adorable.

I lean closer, brushing my lips over hers with only my thumb between us. "Go out on a date with me," I coax.

She whimpers.

I drop my thumb—my lips touch hers for the smallest fraction of a second before she flushes and drops her head, and I lower my hand, giving her room.

"I can't. I need to work," she whispers.

Can't even breathe right, I'm so lust-ridden. I just want to taste those lips some more. Taste all of her.

She's beet red now and turned around to give me her back. I'm watching her fidget with stuff on the desk. "Let's meet after work. Before work. I'd say during work, but I'm not sure you'd enjoy greasing irons for fun," I say, my lips hiking up at the corners.

She turns, biting down on her lower lip. "Not really." She laughs nervously, then raises her eyes to meet mine as if it takes great effort to do so. "But you might enjoy helping me lug some boxes at the warehouse."

"Do you need someone to lug boxes at the warehouse?" I ask.

"Actually, yes. Our usuals are spending Easter weekend with their families, and with the upcoming sales—"

"What time do you get in?" I interrupt.

Her eyes drop to my mouth. "Huh?"

"My eyes are up here."

She pulls her eyes up, blushing again.

"What time do you get in to lug boxes?" I insist.

"5 a.m."

"I'll be there."

I grab her jaw and kiss it, and she inhales sharply as I do. I smile and walk away, hearing her call back, "Thank you. But IT'S NOT A DATE!"

specks

Bryn

I wake up with a throbbing head and pray that I didn't say what I am pretty sure I said to Aaric last night. About my V card. About possibly wanting to have given it to him.

Ohmigod.

I'm not getting a loan now.

I'm not getting another meeting ever again; I'm sure of it.

I need a distraction or I'll do nothing all day but kick myself in the foot for last night. So I quickly shower and change, ready to cajole Sara to go out with me, when Sara raps on my door.

"Bryn? Christos is outside looking for you."

"What?" I open the door, blinking, and right behind her, standing in my living room...

is Aaric.

He looks incredible. He's freshly showered, wearing black jeans and a black, long-sleeve crewneck, his features chiseled and perfect.

"Checking up to see if I'm working?" I tease.

I'm just nervous that he's *here*.

"That's right." He winks and plunges his hands into his pockets, watching me. "Want to go for a walk?"

He picks up two Starbucks coffees from the counter and brings me one, his gaze sparkling.

I swallow, hating that he's probably remembering everything I said last night. I realize Sara is gaping, and I take the coffee nervously and add, "I'd love to take a walk."

He heads to the door and opens it for me. "Nice meeting you," he tells Sara, and Sara shoots me a wide-eyed "my heart!" look.

I shut the door quickly behind me and we head downstairs, then outside, to a gorgeous fall morning.

"We won't talk about last night," I warn as we head out of my apartment.

He shoots me a puzzled look, then hisses under his breath, "*Shit.* Something happened? I can't believe I missed it." He drags a hand across his jaw as if truly disappointed, and I catch on pretty fast.

I laugh, relieved. "Thank you."

His smile deepens for a moment. He sips from his coffee. "So, how are you liking Manhattan?"

I scan the busy streets as we head to SoHo. "I couldn't sleep the first two weeks. I felt over-stimulated, all the traffic, the pedestrians, the noise, things to do, the lights and the life." I grin. "It's a jungle."

He winks down at me.

"Not for the faint of heart," I continue.

He just smiles.

"But now, I'm becoming addicted," I add. "I can't go to sleep without walking the streets every night. I'm enjoying the cool evenings. Now, I find the city exciting." I eye him. "Do you ever miss home?"

He stares thoughtfully ahead, the sun glinting in his hair. "Austin never felt like home to me. I suppose because we moved there for only a few years—no reason for me to stay there after Mother passed."

"I'm sorry about your mom. I'm sorry you left."

"Yeah, well." He tosses his coffee into the trash, shrugging casually and then smiling, slow and wolfish. "You were one of the few reasons I'd hoped to stay."

"But...?" I prod.

"But you didn't deserve some grease monkey." He shoots me a stern look, as if I'm to blame for his success. "You missed me," he states.

"So much I couldn't sleep at night," I exaggerate, rolling my eyes.

"So much you're blushing right now. So you did miss me?" He looks pleased.

I laugh. "Well, I'm blushing because it's true, I missed you. I bet you hardly thought of me after leaving."

"You'd lose that bet." His voice lowers, becoming husky.

Thudthudthud.

I hide my reaction by taking a sip of my coffee. And then another, and one more.

We end up heading to Chelsea, walking along the streets, window shopping as we talk.

I pause and peer into the art galleries, admiring the paintings inside. "I'd miss New York now, if I had to go back. Even though I arrived during the summer, the heat, the smelly trashcans, you can't get over a city like this."

"The stench sucks in summer. Better in fall."

"Everything is better in fall. Even the fashion." I motion to the passersby. "I love the fashion here—it's so varied."

He follows my hand motion, and I pray he doesn't notice the way I'm trying to divert my attention—away from how approachable he feels right now, so tall and warm, so infinitely Aaric Christos. My *what if.*

"I typically don't notice," he says, eyeing me. He stops walking and rakes his gaze over me, his eyes narrowing even more as his lips curve playfully, his quiet gaze telling me he definitely noticed what I'm wearing now.

Lungs, are you doing okay over there?

"Is that one of yours?" He motions to my cutout jeans and a top I made out of two tops—a layered look, sewn strategically in place.

"Yes, well, the jeans are normal jeans but…I made the cuts on the knee. I reassembled this shirt from two old shirts I had, overlaying them. I…" I realize he's looking down at me, and blush. "I'm not sure you'll want the details of that."

"I'm sure I don't mind listening to you talk about it." He smirks, and tilts his head back. To get a better look at my destruction.

"What is the purpose of these cuts?" He motions to the cuts on my legs.

Body! Calm down, please! "I…well, I suppose showing a little skin is never a bad thing." I'm breathing too hard.

He reaches down, frowning, and strokes his thumb along the bare skin of my knee. "Bad for whom? The wearer or the looker?" He straightens, his expression puzzled.

"I...suppose both. The wearer has the pleasure of...well, feeling some air against her skin and of...possibly feeling some attention she may crave coming her way."

"And the looker...?"

My lungs and heart and stomach are all in chaos mode.

"Well, the looker will find...something to look at he may find interesting...that may have more under the surface."

He looks down my legs, then up to my face.

"Clothes aren't just about getting dressed," I continue breathlessly. "They're about expressing yourself, who you are, and setting the stage for how you want to be treated, how you want to be seen."

He shoves his hands into his pockets and stares straight ahead. "You're saying you have control over the way you're seen by others depending on the way you present yourself."

"Yes. I am." I nervously flip my hair back as we start walking again, the air between us so charged I can't believe it's not the focal point of a lightning bolt. "Say I'm wearing comfortable clothes so I just want to be feeling comfortable, treated friendly," I explain. "Maybe if I want to be treated more sensually, I'd wear a short dress, with cleavage, something that sends out the message of what I want from...well, from the party I'm seeing."

"You didn't mean to seduce whoever you were seeing today with this little outfit?" He shoots me a black, rather stark look.

"No! Of course not, it's my most simple."

"I don't buy this." The angle of his jaw squares a little as he clenches it.

"I...honestly!" I laugh.

"You weren't intending to drive some guy's thoughts fucking crazy, Miss Kelly? Wondering what's under there?" he demands disbelievingly, tugging on my top with a playful smile.

"Christos, are you teasing me?!"

"You're teasing the world, bit. This whole outfit is teasing the world."

"Come on!" I laugh hysterically, shaking my head in denial. "I was going dog walking later today," I defend.

"Dogs and babies. Isn't that an age-old trick?"

"Why? Have *you* used it?" I tease. "Is that how you snatched Miranda Santorini?"

His smile fades—and so does mine.

I could bite my tongue for saying that, ugh.

I fidget with my empty coffee cup, and he suddenly takes it from my hand and throws it into a trashcan we pass.

Silence falls between us. I bear a heavy sensation in my chest at the thought of him walking me back home at some point later on.

"You know, I cried when you left," I whisper, glancing at my feet.

His eyes begin shimmering as we share a sideways look, and he looks so gorgeous right now, I would snap a picture of him if I could. "You got my only good shirt wet," he says, looking amused.

"Ohmigod. I'm sorry."

"I'm not. I didn't want it to dry." He brushes his thumb over my cheek, and I laugh to hide the way my whole body burns and fizzles under his touch.

Trying to suppress my reaction, I tell him, "You're a player."

He looks at me in feigned surprise. "I'm not. I swear I'm not."

"You play the game well."

He laughs, shaking his head as we keep walking. Block after block. "It's never been a game with you."

"What are you doing now?" I narrow my eyes, confused.

But truth be told, I want him to keep going. I never want him to stop teasing me. Looking at me like that, with that playful gleam, like a man who knows his effect and doesn't hesitate to use it.

"What am I doing now?" He frowns thoughtfully and glances straight ahead. "Walking down memory lane, in the middle of..."—he glances at the street sign—"20th Street."

I smile, wringing my hands as we keep walking, just two people in a humongous city. I'm sure he's used to this city, but I'm not. I walk in it to remind myself of my size in the grand scope of things, a tiny speck in this galaxy.

I walk this city to see what people do here, talk about here, what they wear, if they look sad or happy. Every single one of us with a dream, all of us shuffling to our destinations, all of us trying to make our experiences here in the world more worthwhile.

Successes, love...the things that make it all intoxicating.

I cannot think of a more intoxicating moment I've experienced in New York so far than walking it with him.

Intoxicating him.

My what if.

I don't want it to end, but I'm aware of it ending with every step we take back in the direction of my apartment.

"Thank you for checking up on me," I say, glancing down to avoid his perceptive eyes noticing my disappointment that our time together didn't last a whole life.

I turn away and hear his voice.

"Bryn." The way he says my name causes a pleasant tremor down my legs as he stops at the door. "There's a dinner I'm hosting next weekend on Saturday evening. I'd like you to meet some important people. People that can eventually help—store owners, designers, marketers. Wear one of your pieces—look like a million bucks. Got it?"

I grin, my heart taking a record leap in my chest. "Got it."

yoga

Bryn

"Push up into down dog," the teacher says.

I go on all fours and lift my ass in a pyramid when I hear Sara whisper, "I saw him in the paper this morning. Did you see the socials section?"

"No. I've got better things to do," I say, moving into cobra pose.

"I bet you do," she snickers, pulling her legs behind her. "Your hotshot real estate tycoon is in there."

Thud. "Right. Like he's not everywhere anyway."

"Silence!" we hear.

My eyes widen and fly to the teacher, and I purse my lips and continue my yoga flow. It's really hard to find my zen with Sara nudging me.

"Apparently, the woman he's dating is some rich socialite. Her hands were all over him and he looked like stone. Like he was literally made of stone."

"I really don't want to talk about him," I beg. I need a distraction, anything to keep me from getting hung up on this bit of information. Anything to keep from searching for him online. Anything to keep from thinking about him. And the fact that he's with another woman.

I had my chance, and I wasn't ready for him then.

And now he's moved on. He's a powerful businessman. All I have is a chance to do business with him, and I'm barely holding onto that. So far, he's started vetting me, but I still haven't gotten a formal yes. Or a check.

He's a risk taker, but even then, he's not yet taking the risk on me.

Not that I didn't blow it getting drunk and talking about V cards and shit! Ugh. I've emailed with him some information on my plan, but he's been curt and businesslike in his responses. Simply "received" or "got it" or "thanks."

I'm afraid I've fucked this up royally!

"You really don't want to talk about him?" she asks seriously.

"No."

"Why?"

"Because"—I pause as the teacher glances at me and wait for her to look away—"I can't stop thinking about having sex with him."

Sara bursts out laughing.

"Ladies!" the teacher barks.

I smile and bite down on my tongue, struggling to remain silent for the rest of the hour.

"Apparently they're speculating an engagement soon," she says as we roll up our mats at the end of class.

"Oh."

"See…" She grabs her phone and scrolls through some pictures. "That's him a year ago. Dubbed the most eligible NY bachelor. Now they're saying she may have snagged him for good." She swipes the screen.

"Then this was taken last week."

I look at the photo. He's at some sort of posh black-tie event, his blonde at his side laying a hand on his chest as if she's claiming him.

My stomach aches.

She tucks the phone back into her pocket as we head to the showers. "If you want him, you need to move *fast*."

"I'm not making a move. We're going to be in business together."

"He hasn't made you pick…business or pleasure, has he?" Sara challenges with a quirked brow. "Have both!"

"I cannot have both, so stop with this talk. You talk sex all day only because you're starved for it."

"No, you know I'm not. I had sex with the sexiest man alive but since I haven't been able to figure out his name, I'm saving myself until I find him again."

I glance at her. "Do you really not know his name? How long ago was this?"

"A few months. His room was booked under a company name. They always send different executives. I *really* don't know his name. But that's all right. I bet he can't top it a second time. If I can't find him, then I'd rather keep the memory."

For a moment she looks wistful, and I realize Sara is actually *really* into this one-night-stand guy.

"See? You've gone celibate, so now you're trying to make me act like a slut?"

"*Christ* doesn't want me. If he wanted me, I'd be all over that."

"Christ-*os*," I correct. "And I should never have told you the story," I tell her. "It wasn't like he proposed or professed undying love for me. We were in high school. He was just…interested. And I was scared. It's been forever now. The end."

Sara shrugs and we undress, get our towels, and step into the showers. I place myself under the spray, and I picture Aaric touching my bare skin, his mouth tasting me. I dislike the fact that I'm thinking about it, thinking of him. I have my own issues to deal with. I can't sleep without setting off alarm clocks every two hours in case of a fire. I'm afraid to love because losing the closest people in my life was devastating enough. I can't risk it. One more loss would destroy me.

Aaric is hardworking, relentless, and gorgeous, but even if he were single, I'm not sure I'd have the courage to go for it. Not with my business also on the line. Not with my heart on the line. So I try not to think of sexy things, like how his lips would feel on mine.

What it would feel like to be the woman on his arm.

I push that thought away and madly scrub shampoo into my scalp.

"Wear something tight tonight. I'm pretty sure guys equate the tighter the dress with the tighter the pussy."

"That's seriously not why they like tight dresses."

"Well, it's a good theory. Who knows what they think? Maybe your friend Becka knows."

"How do you know Becka?"

"You told me about her. She's in Austin writing a sexy book. Right? Rebecca?"

"True. I'll ask her if you can read it now that you seem so interested," I say, tongue-in-cheek.

"Girl, I need *no* sexy books in my life if I'm not getting any sexy. What do you want to do with me, make me tackle the doorman?"

"We don't have a doorman."

"That's right, but the building across from us does." She smirks.

"Oh, Sara." I laugh and head into my closet, trying to keep the laughter alive and ignore how nervous I am about this meeting with Aaric.

She's right though. I should definitely ask Becka to let me read her stuff in private late at night or I'll end up tackling Aaric Christos.

you, there

Christos

13 years ago...

"**H**ey. You there, mechanic boy? Come fix my car," some douchebag yells.

I'm bent over a hood when something hits me on the shoulder. I glance at my shoulder, then at the floor, where a banana peel has fallen.

I raise my head to find some dude giving me shit. I give him the finger before I notice something move next to him.

Bryn Kelly.

My stomach freezes. She smiles at me apologetically from the front seat.

I don't smile.

Hell, I can't stand to see her with him.

I keep working, but the asshole won't take no for an answer.

"Hey. You. Fix my car now? I have a hot date waiting."

"Kyle, stop," she hisses angrily.

I slam the hood closed. She jumps a little. I look at her, then at him, and walk forward.

I knock on his hood. "Open up," I say.

He does. "Now we're talking," he says, clearly pleased.

I lean over, fiddle with the cables, and slam it closed. "We're done."

"How much do I owe you?" He counts his bills.

"On the house." I smirk as I walk back to the shop then watch him through the corner of my eye as he tries to start it. Nothing happens. "Asshole. I just needed the oil changed. Now it won't fucking start!"

I grab a cloth and wipe my fingers as I head back to the vintage I'm working on. From under the hood, I hear him ranting.

"I'll fucking sue you! I'll sue you for your damned life!"

Bryn has hopped out and is on the phone. Ten minutes later, her father picks her up. She opens the door to his truck and raises her head to look at me. I stop working and watch her.

I watch the way she climbs into the car, the way she nervously explains what happened to her dad, and the way she looks at me before they drive off.

As they pull away, she smiles to herself. A sweet, shy smile I feel all the way down to my goddamned testicles.

Moron Kyle charges forward. "You got a hard-on for Bryn Kelly?"

I say nothing. Bend back over my work.

He's trying to pick a fight, but I've got better things to do.

"She's too good for you." He spits on the motor.

I straighten, grab my rag, and wipe it off. He slams inside to speak to the manager. I can get fired—but I know I won't be. I work weekends, I work nights, I work for free. I work to forget my mom is sick and my future and Cole's looks like shit. I work because I'm good at it. But despite myself, I frown from irritation.

Because this girl I want? She *is* too good for me. But I've got plans, and a shit ton of ambition, and if I have my way—which I plan to—I won't always be a grease monkey.

One day, I'll own the land morons like this walk on.

s.o.b

Bryn

want to make a good impression on him and I really think
being free to mingle will be the way to go, so I arrive at the
dinner scene dateless, with a backless dress that I cut up
and sewed myself, and a gung-ho attitude that quickly takes a
hit when I say my name at the door and step in.

Classical music plays in the background, and I'm instantly impressed by the edgy, simple floral arrangements and
chrome banquet tables.

It's not a huge event. But the kind of people here aren't
numerous in the world to begin with. Two hundred of the most
elite, rich, high-powered movers and shakers in the city. From
bankers (I recognize some) to marketers, to successful business sharks like my possible investor himself.

I feel a prick on the back of my neck, and when I turn,
he's there. He's seated at a table next to a couple, and I feel my
breath snag in my throat when I realize he's looking at me. His
expression pensive. His eyes curious.

I try not to notice how hot he looks in his gray suit with his hair slicked back away from his forehead. A black button shirt and no tie. He smiles at something the couple says and looks away for a second, and I quickly turn around and try to find a glass of wine.

I'm going to need it tonight.

"Hey, babe."

I glance at the purple-haired man with a drink in his hand. He looks like he's an artist. Long hair in a ponytail, eyes a little red. I think he's stoned.

"Want a drink?" he asks.

"The one you spiked, amigo? No, thanks." I turn away when he grabs my arm to spin me around back to face him.

"How would you know if you haven't even taken a sip, feisty? Come on, don't be like that," he says in an obvious attempt to be charming. "We're here to mingle. Get to know each other. Aren't we?" He winks. "I'm Yael—the brains behind every successful campaign you see everywhere."

My heart skips when I feel the warmth of a body behind me. A pleasant scent of soap envelops me, and my stomach clutches when I recognize the smell. Nobody else would have this effect on me.

I feel his fingers on the small of my back and his voice so close to my ear that the warmth of his breath spills along the back of my neck. "I see you've met Yael," he says.

I feel myself blush and nod.

"Did you go overboard on the coke tonight?" Christos asks him.

"Just following my heart." He grins.

"Follow my advice—take it down a notch."

"Christos," the man says, sobering up instantly. "Come on. I was nervous, all right? I want your gigs."

"I invited you here to show my partners what you have to offer—I regret you didn't decide to bring your best to the table." He nods at me. "He's still good. You might consider him in the future. If you'll excuse us, Yael."

I inhale as he moves me away. "That was harsh," I say and reach out impulsively to take the glass of wine from his hand. His fingers accidentally touch mine. A million tingles race up my fingertip and arm, making me want to rub the touch away.

Please God, I don't need this complication.

I down the wine, frowning up at him as he frowns down at me.

"What?"

"I told you to look like a million bucks."

"What?" I gasp, blinking in shock as he grins—slowly, predatorily.

This man is lethal. His face isn't spoiled by too much beauty, only chiseled angles and masculine features. It's very attractive. More than a perfect face, its imperfection stuns you. Everyone seems to stare at it—at *him*.

He leans forward. "You seem to have mistaken your millions with billions, Wicked Miss Kelly."

He winks, and all the heat in the world settles inside my stomach.

"Are you all right to mingle?"

"Yes," I say.

He leaves me and spends the night talking to everyone but me.

He's clearly the most powerful man in the room, but his attitude is calm. He's in control, subdued, even though his energy is a pulsing, magnetizing, electric thing noticeable from far away.

I try to ignore it as I make my way through the room, introducing myself to people. "Are you working with Christos?" I'm asked.

"I...well. I might be." I don't know what to say. I mean, he's been asking. He's seemed interested.

That's when I realize he's got other people here, people like me, whom he's prioritizing with his introductions. I start to stew.

He sends me a smile across the room.

And that's that.

I start getting really pissed off.

I exhale and try to head outside to get some air when he follows me. I don't even reach the doors when I feel him behind me and I whirl around.

"You son of a bitch, you're playing with me. You're not interested in my business!"

He raises his brows. "I am."

"Why did you even bring me here? I don't know what to answer when people ask me about our business. MY business. Which may not even see the light of day."

"Do you really believe it won't?"

I purse my lips.

He takes me by the chin. "You're the most amazing woman I've ever known. I have every confidence you're not only going to get on your feet. You'll fly."

"If you believe that much in me, *prove* it. Say yes. Give me the money. Do *something*!" I croak out.

His eyes lose their sparkle, and in its stead, a blazing gold hue takes over them as he reaches into his pocket. Ever so slowly, he pulls out a check. "I was planning to give it to you at the end of the night."

He stares me down as he hands it over: a check with my name on it and a six-digit figure.

I cannot believe what I'm staring at.

My hand trembles as I take it from him. I fold it in half and tuck it into my purse, my throat raw. "Thank you. I...I'm sorry I overreacted..."

I want to cry. Nobody's done anything like this for me. I blink and move away, heading to the restroom.

I splash water on my face, then pat it dry and hasten to go back out. Christos is standing with Cole, and that same woman they were sitting with when I arrived is standing with them too.

"Hey, little lady," Cole says.

"Hi and bye, Cole," I say, smiling as I hug him.

"You're leaving?"

I nod. "I've got some business cards and I'm inspired to brainstorm with myself now that Christos said yes." I smile nervously, and Cole frowns.

"Sugar, being invited here is an automatic yes," he says, as if it's obvious.

I feel heat on my cheeks as I realize I must have sounded like a desperate idiot to Christos just now. "Well, it's official," I say, still avoiding Aaric's gold gaze. "And he won't regret it. Well, goodnight!" I nod at all three of them when I hear Christos's gruff voice.

"*He*," he specifies, "will take you home." He reaches for his jacket on the back of the chair.

"Oh no, I'll take the train. Thank you. Goodnight."

"I insist," he says, warning. Low.

He puts on his jacket and grabs his cell phone from the table.

I pause, breathless when our eyes meet as he pockets his phone. It's as if he knows I was having a moment in the ladies' bathroom. "I don't want you to go out of your way," I breathe.

"I won't." He nods down at me, his voice a little tender.

Cole notices something off for his tone changes too.

"I'll drop off Therese," Cole interjects.

"Thank you, goodnight," Aaric says noncommittally, putting his hand on the small of my back as he leads me outside.

We head for his car. I'm trembling. He puts his arm around me and pins me to his side.

I press closer.

His little act of kindness makes me feel accepted—understood. I feel as if he sees me, and it causes me to come unhinged.

I slide into his car when he opens the door for me, despite my previous efforts to avoid it. I thought it would feel intimate and it does. He's a powerful, attractive man and I'm only human.

I smell the leather of the car and Aaric as he slides in behind me, shuts the door, and tells his driver his Park Avenue address.

The car heads into traffic.

I turn, and he cups my jaw and presses his lips to mine.

first sight

Christos
14 years ago...

"**H**e's the new guy. The older one. He was held back for two years because his mom is sick."

I slam my locker shut, aware of the speculations around me and Cole.

I scan the halls for my class when I spot the back of a girl's head, and my eyes lock on it. On her. The girl who was at the shop last weekend with her dad.

My chest feels heavy. My legs, thighs, every muscle in my body is ready to pounce. I hesitate for a second, aware of the curious gazes on me, then I charge forward and catch up with her and her friend.

"Hi," I say, my voice a little lower than I expected. "I'm Aaric."

"Bryn," she says in return, a blush on her cheeks.

She turns away to head off with her friend, but when she opens the door to her room, she glances back at me with a smile on her face.

I stare at her. Bryn.

I don't know what it is, but I can't take my eyes away from her. The way she looks. The way she walks. The way she smiles. The way she talks.

The solar-plexus punching, gut-wrenching, bucket-of-water feeling of seeing my future in her eyes.

business

Bryn

His tongue flicks into my mouth, and it's as if the whole universe is opening up to swallow me. I feel helpless to stop it, this sensation of being devoured as his mouth opens and his tongue plunges in—hot, wet, greedy.

A soft moan escapes me, and a shudder of warmth wracks me head to toe as I reach out to slip my fingers in his hair. He groans hungrily, grabbing me by the back of the neck and holding me in place as he presses his thumb to my lips and eases back to look at me.

He looks devastated.

As if I just gave him food for the first time in his life.

He murmurs *fuck me* under his breath and rubs his thumb over my mouth—like he did once, at Kelly's. Then he presses his mouth to his thumb and sets his forehead on mine, waiting...

I meet his gaze and pant wildly in shock. I want to open my mouth, but I know I shouldn't. I am not sure if *he* knows that he shouldn't.

But, *fuck me* too, because oh, how I *want*. I want to crawl out of my skin and into him, if only to get rid of the fire burning every inch of me. I want everything this guy can give me. Things no one in my life has ever given me. Forbidden things that scare me, thrill me, churn a crazy wild fire inside me. Bryn the Good Girl wants out, and Bryn the One Who Doesn't Play It Safe wants in.

Christos is taken. He's completely wrong and it doesn't even matter. He's the last man you'd take home to your parents because he doesn't belong to you—because even when you knew he wanted you, you feared he'd never belong to you.

But I want him. No, I don't want to marry the guy, or even date the guy. I want his hands on me. His mouth on me. I want it raw and hard, but I'm afraid for him to know it.

I'm afraid to even want it.

I've seen him with his girlfriend, and he's never looked at her with the warmth he looks at me. I'm shocked to realize I'm selfish, terrible, because at this moment nothing is as important as the fact that I want his hands on me.

I stay in place, motionless, and feel his thumb push a little bit upward, then a little bit downward, opening my mouth and then...

Fuck us both, because his mouth is covering both my top and bottom lips and his tongue is covering the tiny space in between, widening the part and going in.

I get caught up in it, in him, in how right it feels, in how 14 years could have never happened because he is still *him*. I'm swept away by all of what really happened and dive into my *what if*...tasting him back. He's moving his head, this way and that, never once taking his lips away from mine, groaning when my own tongue, thirsty and reckless and thoughtless, comes out to rub his. Taste his.

He kisses a thousand times better than in my decade-long fantasies. So good my heart beats in my whole body—my chest, my stomach, my thighs, in between...

The car jolts to a stop, and I jolt back—blinking again as I try to place myself.

I can't believe I'd ever be this girl. That I'd kiss a guy who had a girlfriend, but I know it would never happen with any guy. Only *this* guy.

Christos sits up with an exhale that causes his nostrils to flare, and he pulls me up while I slowly come back to reality.

I take a look at his lips, and feel a knot of guilt build up in my stomach and my throat.

The stern look on his face is wholly intimidating—he's either rethinking what he did or determined to do it again.

I'm pinned in place, not moving a muscle. Grappling to come to terms with what I just did.

How I just...*lost control.*

With Aaric.

Aaric Christos.

Even when he has a girl. Even when I have his check in my purse. Even when I know now, for sure, that we'll be doing business together.

Ohmigod, I'm a bad person.

I'm so bad, so bad.

This is bad.

The driver opens his door, and Aaric buttons his suit jacket as he comes to full height, glancing at me one last time. He wears no tie, as if he couldn't be bothered.

"Come on, bit," he says as he draws me out of the car.

I swallow nervously and twine my fingers together, trying to walk calmly toward his front door. Just breathe. But it's hard to breathe when my whole life has been spectacular plus spectacular fall and he's the only constant in it. I feel the loss of his body heat as we walk, inches between us, up his brownstone. But I don't want to go home yet. I want my friend Aaric right now. I need his presence like I need air.

He opens the door with his key, then leads me inside, to a living room with a view of the most perfect garden.

I walk along the room, inspecting the shelves—trying to put some distance between us and pretend things are back like they were before…that kiss.

He's got a minimalist thing going on with very few items on the shelves—but each piece is striking. I stop before a large obelisk in a crystal white shade; the object looks as if it's a piece of the moon itself.

"This is beautiful. What is this?"

"It's a rare piece of quartz. One side is smoky quartz, the other clear quartz. It's so pure you can see right through it."

"It's gorgeous. A collectible. The kind on auction catalogues."

He smirks—and I realize that's where he got it.

"And this?" I point at another stone. "You got this at an auction too?" At his silence, I shoot him a disgruntled look. "Can you tell me something you didn't get at auction?"

He removes his jacket and sets it aside. "I can't recall."

"God, are you interested in *nothing* where there's no competition?"

"Competition makes every item here look all the better in my place."

He smiles, and I'm laughing. "This?" I point at a pre-Columbian figurine made of jade. "Don't tell me. Auction."

"That was actually a gift." His eyes somber, darken. "My mother gave that to me ages ago. It was part of a ring that belonged to her grandmother."

It's a small thing, set in an acrylic base, which summarizes its importance to its owner.

"Tell me about her."

"She was very strong, very dedicated. She fought very hard to live. She was never ready to go, not even in the last minute."

"She waved at me through the window, the few times I walked by." I stare out the window, watching the streets outside.

He's near—behind me. I sense him like a boiler of hot water standing close to me, and I almost don't move for fear of being scorched.

"Are we going to talk about it?" he whispers, in my ear, slipping his hand around my waist.

"I don't know."

I turn and meet his gaze.

"Are you going to marry her?"

He looks down at me with the barest shadow of surprise in his expression over my question. "I'm 32 years old. I want a family of my own." He narrows his eyes, tilting his head—rubbing my lips with his thumb.

"You do?"

He nods. "Never had a family. Not a traditional one. Just because I didn't have a father doesn't mean I don't want to be one. I do."

"With her? What if she's not the one?"

"In marrying her, I'd be committing to her being the one even if it's not a love match—and she would do the same with me. Isn't that the point of getting the government involved?"

"What if you love someone else, and someone else loves you? What if you want to take someone else to bed, and she wants to take you?"

He's silent.

His thumb on my mouth. Rubbing side to side.

"Why did you bring me here?"

"You seemed upset. I didn't want you to be alone to-night." He drops his hands and plunges them deep into his pockets as he looks at me, his voice becoming lower and deep-er. "And I didn't want to be without you tonight."

I glance away, then back at him. "Thank you for believing in me," I whisper.

"Thank you for bringing something to the table that's worth pursuing," he counters, his gaze direct. "I gave you the check because I want us to do business together. Don't think for a moment I don't."

"That kiss was business too?"

He smirks. "No. That was for me."

Squirming under my skin from the heat sizzling in the space between our bodies, I run my hands down my dress. "I won't lie and say I haven't thought about you and I. But it's complicated. You're in a relationship and we're starting a business partnership. I'm not the kind of girl that goes stealing men from other girls."

"I'm not stealable." He grins.

"What does that mean?"

He just looks at me for a long moment. "Sleep with me."

"Is that a good idea?" I gasp in disbelief at his suggestion. "I can hardly keep my hands to myself right now."

"Spend the night with me," he says.

"Aaric."

He takes my chin and lifts my face, one eyebrow rising. "We can talk business."

I swallow.

"Or we can actually sleep," I hedge.

"I'm up for that." His lips hike up halfway as he nods in consent.

"We can't kiss again," I breathe.

His gaze falls to my mouth. Is there regret there? Lust? Both? "I'm trying to take it slow with you, Bryn."

"Christos...frankly, I don't know what to make of this."

"Like I said, I'm hoping to take it slow enough for you to feel comfortable."

"Comfortable with what?"

"The idea of you and me being involved, bit. To us taking things to where we want them. Tonight I want you to sleep here—I can sleep in a separate room if you need your space."

"I don't want space. But I don't want to regret any-thing..." I trail off.

Because I already know sometimes the regrets go both ways. Going home won't guarantee that I won't wake up with-out any regrets. With more what ifs, more mind-dream kisses from Christos.

"I suppose if I'm staying I should change. Do you have something decent I can wear?" I ask.

We walk into his bedroom—it's too big and beautifully decorated to be anything but his. He leads me to the closet, motioning to the very end.

I am surprised to find a whole section of his closet contains women's things. I would leave if he weren't standing at the door watching me. "I'm not wearing Miranda's stuff."

"She leaves shit here. Grab anything else." He pushes off the door frame.

"I'm not wearing her stuff!" I raise my voice so he can hear me as I stalk to the other side of his closet, undo my dress, then quickly grab a folded gray sweatshirt and slip my arms into the sleeves.

He stands by the bed and watches me walk into his room while he fiddles with his phone. His head snaps back attentively, and he freezes.

"What?" I ask.

He stares another moment longer.

"Just really like seeing you in my things," he says. Low. A lovely smirk on his lips.

I smile, flushing head to toe.

"1 a.m., right?" he asks, glancing down at his phone.

I realize what he is doing and discreetly bite down on my lip while more heat bubbles up in my veins. I nod.

He sets his phone aside and pulls back the sheets in invitation.

He's still dressed. I'm wearing nothing but my undergarments and his very large sweatshirt and his eyes on me—eyes that won't focus on anything else.

God. He makes me feel sexy and that's dangerous. I already feel sensitive when it comes to him. And I've never done something like this. This is a little too brazen for me, but I still cross the room and settle into his bed. I have no intention of misbehaving, but the truth is…

I don't want to sleep alone tonight either.

He unbuttons his shirt, revealing his tattoo. It runs up over his shoulders and across part of his chest.

I'm no longer relaxed. Not one bit.

He climbs the bed with me, I hold my breath.

I feel his bare chest against me as he draws me toward him. His long legs still in slacks.

"I'm going to regret this tomorrow, aren't I?" I cant my head up to his and shift to get closer.

"No." His mouth presses to my forehead, and that tiny contact makes me groan. "God, I want to feast on you," he says, against my temple.

His eyes gleam as he slips his hand to my hair and squeezes the back of my neck proprietarily as he ducks his head and takes my mouth beneath his, the kiss so hard and brazen it pushes the back of my head into the pillow and my senses into chaos.

I feel myself claw at his scalp and his fingers fist my hair, the kiss full of tongue and teeth and frustration and lust.

Six minutes later or a lifetime later, we stop kissing. My mouth hurts like hell, but I still want more. He looks ready to turn to ash from the heat in his gaze as he takes in my expression.

He looks about as wrecked as I feel, because I'm stealing this moment from him. A moment that should belong to another girl.

He looks wrecked but hungry, so hungry that when he ducks his head for another kiss, I turn my head and breathe, "We can't. We can't do this." He lets out a soft but frustrated laugh and whispers in the back of my ear, "We can. But I'll wait for you, Bryn. I'll wait to get any piece of you I can get."

It's almost enough to break my resolve.

morning after

Bryn

It felt surreal to wake up at his place at 1 a.m.

At 3 a.m.

at 5 a.m.

and at 7 a.m.

The first three times, he turned off the alarm and whispered in my ear that I was okay. For some reason, I believed him and went back asleep. At 7 a.m., a different sound began buzzing. The clock on the nightstand.

I scanned his empty bedroom in a panic.

Did I really sleep here?

I breathe, spot a note on his pillow, and get out of bed.

I consider using the shower, but then rule against it. When I return his sweatshirt to the drawers, I can't help but peek at the long line of female things in his closet. The clothes Miranda has left here. They are made of high-quality fabrics. I don't want to do this to myself. In fact, I'm not going to compare. It's ridiculous to think she's the better woman because of her clothes, because she wears European designer and I wear my own, and I know it's not true. But I can't help but remember what Christos told me. They make sense as a couple—and in the light of day they make more sense. Last night seems more reckless and impulsive than ever.

This is just not who I am!

Proof of how much this guy gets to me.

Once back in my clothes, I pull out his note and read it.

Coffee in the kitchen. Meet me at 1 p.m. tomorrow at C & Co. I want you in the board of directors meeting to introduce them to HOS.

Christos.

I shut my eyes.

Oh God, how can I face him?

"Hey. Hankypankier," Sara says when I get to our flat. It's a sunny morning, and as I get off the train and walk to the apartment building, the streets are back to its usual Monday hectic pace.

"Hey." I drop my bag on the small dining table and head to the bathroom to turn on the shower.

"No hanky panky?" Sara calls as I join her while I wait for the water to get hot.

"No, so you can stop calling me hankypankier."

"Oh." She brings me a cup of coffee. "Is it the tycoon?"

"No. It's…well, yes. He's my new business partner now. So hanky panky isn't really a good idea. Last night I was just…I just had an emotional breakdown, a little one. I thought he was playing around with me. Then he gave me the check and I felt like a fool…and I felt grateful, and it just…brought his memories back up again. It was a weird night. It's over. Now I'm all business." I *have* to be.

"He gave you all the money?"

I meet her startled gaze. I feel just as shocked as she looks. Is my startup really going to happen? Am I really going to be able to dress people, help them choose their outfits with minimal effort, and design my own things? "More than I was asking for. I need to spend it better than ever. Do you want to model?"

"Excuse me?"

"Do you want to model—"

"When and where."

"Soon. I need to talk to Christos, but I'll tell you more when he gives me a green light on everything."

On Monday, I present my ideas to the board, with Christos— quiet, sexy, dangerous-to-me Christos—at the head of the table.

My legs tremble as he gazes at me.

He's dressed in plain gray slacks and a white shirt, and he looks as untouchable as ever. I can't believe the things we do in the night when we feel like there will never be daylight again.

Oh God. Could I have not gone home on my own instead? Please?

"House of Sass is a brand-new concept," I tell the group of twelve men seated at the long mahogany oak table. "Embracing the traditional as well as the modern-day woman who shops online more than at physical stores. We aim to meet both needs—with fashion stylists in-store and with our avant-garde software aimed to give women an edge to dress to impress and step into the roles of their dreams more easily..."

Christos scans his board members' reactions before he returns his gaze to me.

My blood feels thick as oil in my veins when I remember the way his mouth moved over mine. I was so undone. So worried that he's with another woman, that it's wrong.

I look at him across the table, quiet, simmering with tightly leashed energy.

He looks like a man who's physically enjoyed life, but the hard lines on his features makes me wonder if he's ever loved anyone. Mentally, emotionally, with his soul. And if he's ever been loved back. During all these years apart, I don't think Christos has ever experienced what we could have had together when we were young, and for a moment I feel sorry for us—for him, for me—sorry we didn't experience it. Then I admire him, envy him. For his freedom, the complete fullness of his being, where no pieces have broken off yet. Even when he's with a woman, he's still him—free, unattached in the most essential ways.

Unattached in a way I'm not sure I'm unattached—*from him.*

Once my presentation is over, I thank the board members for their time while Christos steps out with Cole.

I gather my things and overhear them arguing when I step out into the hall. Cole is passionately speaking while Christos stands with his hands in his pockets, his lips pursed tight, and a look of irritation on his face.

"What you did is bad business. Why would you possibly do that? She's very unhappy about that. Plus to get on Santorini's bad side when he owns half of Brooklyn..."

Trying not to overhear more, I hurry to leave when I hear Roberta, Aaric's assistant's, voice behind me.

"Miss Kelly?"

I stop and watch her rush up to my side with a business card in her hand.

"Mr. Christos wants you to meet him tonight at this restaurant. It's in Chelsea. 7 p.m. Sharp."

"Oh...thank you." I raise my gaze past her shoulders, and Christos is still standing before Cole, but his eyes are now on me.

A little trembly, I take the card. I feel a strange tingle in my stomach as I read his handwriting. The top of the card reads FIG & OLIVE. I try to quell the sensation of tumbling down a huge mountain as I send him a smile—the feeling intensifies when he smiles back at me—and I tell myself this is going to be a business dinner. Nothing more. It cannot be more, not for the good of us, our business, or his relationship with the perfect society girl.

fig & olive

Bryn

At 7 p.m., I walk into the restaurant. He's waiting at the entrance, dressed in black jeans and a black shirt, and he watches me as I step through the glass doors.

My mouth waters at his intense, unapologetic, possessive gaze.

"Hey," I say.

He smiles as he leans forward and embraces me. "Glad you came." His eyes shine as if he really is glad.

We're led to our table, and Christos motions for me to follow the maître d'. He lets me slide inside the booth before he takes his seat next to me. Our shoulders connect.

"Hungry?" he asks.

"Yes. But we could have met somewhere less—"

He's so close.

My thoughts scatter.

"Go on," he says.

"Well, it's just that I don't want you to misinterpret what we have for anything other than business. It seemed imperative I see you, and I thought it best to personally tell you that I was out of line. I'm not interested in dating you, but I really appreciate what you've done for me…"

He raises his brow, watching me. His mouth. His face. He's a complete sex god and once, long ago, he was interested in me. I close my eyes as I remember once, when he tried to kiss me. "Got it," he says. "But you are here. And from now until the night is over, you're with me. And I plan to enjoy you."

"Okay, but don't think you can change my mind about you."

"Don't worry, I won't even try. I'm as bad as they say."

His features are completely unreadable as he looks at me, giving me a slow, decadent smile.

Damn him. He looks so gorgeous. I don't want to feel this compelled to act crazy, but he makes me lose all rationale.

I laugh and glance down at the menu, trying not to notice how my left side feels warmer than my right because he's sitting next to me.

I won't go there! I can't help being attracted but I'm not some animal ruled by lust. I can control it. But I'm afraid how the urge to touch him—even if just playfully—keeps coming, how the stares won't stop happening, how this craving inside me won't cease.

"I could tell at the meeting you were upset with me. I didn't like it," he says.

"Not upset. It was just difficult to see you after last night." I exhale, meeting his gaze. "I didn't expect you to help me."

"Why?"

"I don't know. It took me aback after weeks of not knowing. I got overwhelmed. I don't want you to think I spent the night because you gave me the money, it just…reminded me of you. Years ago. Made feelings come up."

"Seeing you on edge made feelings come up for me too."

"Which feelings?"

"The ones I'm pretty sure I was clear about with my tongue."

"And the rest?"

"It's complicated."

He shuts the menu, leaning forward.

"You're not making things easy for me. I always know what I want. Unfuckingwavering. But then you come along."

"And."

"And you change everything." He drags a hand down his face.

"Nothing changes, Christos. We're still going to do business—and you can go on with your life as planned."

"Can I? Really? Let me show you some food while you're starving, but go ahead, keep starving."

"Come on," I laugh.

"Fourteen years starving to kiss you."

My smile fades.

"Do you feel better now?" I whisper.

"I do. Hungrier. But a little better." He eyes me. "There's always been something about you."

"Please. This is complicated enough as it is. I'm trying to focus on House of Sass. I need it to work, and I don't want to fail you."

"You won't," he says. "And you're right. I want you focused." His eyes trail over my features for three seconds too long, then he shakes his head and opens up his phone calendar to show me some notes.

"We need to look at locations for the physical store. Keep an eye out. I'm having my people send you a list of land and buildings I own. Maybe one of those will work."

"Thank you, Christos." I smile shyly. "I found a model in case we require some sort of advertising."

I proceed to tell him about Sara as well as my hopes to maybe have a store more similar to a "showroom" than an actual department store. "People shop online more and more these days, so we can have a showroom warehouse, which can serve as an office space and storage space, to also sell the merchandise. We can also have the servers down in the basement much like you have in Christos and Co."

He seems to like my suggestions, and although I'm glad to be talking about business, I can't help but reach out and occasionally touch his shoulder as I talk, craving the contact.

The rest of the week I scout locations along with some of Christos's employees, who drive me around town to show me possible sites for the House of Sass offices and headline store. I'm given an invitation from Christos and Co. to the opening of one of his newest real estate developments, a 70-story skyscraper apartment building near Columbus Circle. "Thank you, I'll try to make it," I tell her.

"Oh, you'd better. He personalized yours." She winks, and I turn the invitation to once again see his handwriting with the message:

I expect my little bit to come. C

Whoa, my ovaries just exploded a little, and I'm not even sure he phrased it like that on purpose.

Naturally, I cannot stop looking at the invitation during the week, and Sara and I spend a whole two hours one evening speculating on whether—or not—the word "come" had a double meaning.

"I'm telling you he has a girlfriend," I say.

Sara says, "Well, they've been mysteriously off the social pages for a while, and she appeared alone at an event last weekend."

She pulls out an image of Miranda and her father at an event, no Christos.

"That doesn't mean anything," I say. "I'm still taking Jensen. I really don't feel like seeing his blonde at his side, rubbing his chest, calling him darling," I admit, feeling nauseous.

"You want to be the one doing it," Sara jests.

"No!" I say.

"Really?" she taunts me.

I don't know what to tell her—there's no reason for me to be jealous over Christos. It's not as if I truly believe I'm his type, well, at least not anymore, and I've lost too many loved ones to risk my heart—especially with the one guy I've always been afraid could have the power to crush it.

That evening, I take the subway with Jensen and then walk a few blocks to the event. "You look hot, woman. Relax."

"Stop telling me to relax," I whisper.

"Why?"

"Because it reminds me I'm nervous and I'm trying hard to pretend I'm not," I hiss.

We walk into the black granite lobby to an orchestra playing classical music. There are round tables with pristine white linens and silver settings, and buffet tables with beautiful floral arrangements.

I spot Yael and introduce him to Jensen while I head over to do two things: check my makeup for the fifth time tonight and grab something to drink.

Outside the ladies' bathroom, in the hall, I spot Miranda with a brunette talking in hushed tones, oblivious to my presence.

"Wells told me he's got the ring, and I think he'll propose soon. Tonight."

"He won't. It's over," Miranda says.

"What? Why? *When?*"

"Two weeks ago," she huffs angrily. "I didn't tell you because I was sure he'd come to his senses."

"He will. He *has* to. You two make sense. He's usually so levelheaded."

"It's that little tramp from his past! Waving her tiny natural tits at him! I'm telling you, since she appeared, he's been different. It's like he no longer cares about business."

He cares about mine, I want to contradict. *And I'm not a tramp waving my tits!*

She seems to sense me and turns.

"I'd like to use the ladies', if you don't mind," I say, as calmly as possible, pointing at the door.

She looks down her nose at me and brushes past. "If you think you can keep the interest of a man as worldly as Christos…" she warns.

I swallow and head into the ladies', shut and lock the door, and then stare down at the sink, completely forgetting why I'm here.

They broke up. Two weeks ago?

When was it?!

Before he kissed me…

Before…or maybe after…the night he walked me home, when I was drunk out of my mind?

I can't breathe right. I try to tell myself that it doesn't matter. It's not like we're going to get involved in anything.

Are we?

By the time I head out, the room is more crowded than when I arrived, and as I scan the crowd for Jensen—I see him. Aaric.

Looking straight at me.

My knees wobble. The possessiveness in his stare makes me think that this man hasn't forgotten the night I spent at his place either.

There's a tightening between my legs, an uncomfortable feeling. I squirm and shift to get away from his stare.

"He's Aaric Christos."

"Hmm."

Jensen is at my side, amused. "The guy you're staring at—hell, the guy staring at you. He clearly means to have you in his bed sooner than you can say Aaric!"

"Hush. It's not like that." I laugh, moving away.

"Well...he definitely wants it to be like that. He seems to dig you very much." He forces me to turn, and he's still with a group of men—and he's still looking at me with those penetrating eyes that are basically stripping me of every scrap of clothing I'm wearing.

He's smiling this time. Though I'm not sure you could consider that a smile, not even a smirk, it's too subtle for that. Just a slight curving at one corner of his lips—as if he's already doing things to me in his mind.

There's a silence as he approaches, and for a second all I can hear is the roaring sound the harsh pounding of my heart is making in my eardrums.

I turn to leave, determined not to make a fool of myself in front of his snotty ex-girlfriend.

"I'm afraid I can't let you leave just yet."

I raise my brows, as he looks at Jensen with a nod of greeting, then reaches out to place his hand on my shoulder.

"You just stand there and take up the entire room," he says, close to my ear.

"That's in your mind."

"My mind is my whole world."

"Christos." I flush heatedly.

He shoots me a devil's look, and quivering, I edge free and meet his gaze. "I'm not sure I'm welcome here. I'm pretty sure your girlfriend would like to have me shot. I should—"

"You're not leaving."

"I am."

He frowns, glancing at the windows, starting to get wet with rain. "It's pouring outside, bit."

"So?"

"So that's not the kind of wet I wanted to get you," he says with a smirk.

He slides his hand to the small of my back and draws me into the crowd, and I'm rethinking this whole night. "Mingle for a while. I'll find you later tonight. Take you home."

I gulp and nod, confused about what I just learned. Jensen leans into my ear. "Aaric Christos told you he'd find you. Girl, there'll be no place to hide."

"Jensen!"

Aaric is across the room, yet it's a constant struggle to ignore his large, strong hands resting at his sides. My body quivers with wanting to feel them on my skin.

I think of the way we curled together and my blood boils in my veins.

Yael asks me about House of Sass and I try to keep up with the conversation, but Aaric is staring at me.

"I'm interested in working with you," I say. "I respect the fact that you need to get...well, a little..." I give him a look. "To reach your creative nirvana."

He laughs. "I like this girl!" he tells Jensen, and Jensen says, "I like her too."

"Jensen, really." I shoot him a look, then decide I've been here long enough.

I don't want to be rude to Christos, so I approach his group to say my goodbye, aware of him watching every step I take in his direction.

"I'm leaving."

"I'll take you home."

I start saying *no. It's raining. We'll be getting wet.*

"We can talk business," he says. His lips curving.

And I say, *yes.*

"I ended it before last weekend."

We're riding in the back of his car, toward his place. I hold my breath at his words.

"Before we were even in the socials section. She hasn't spread the word out, thinking it's salvageable," he adds.

"Why. Why did you break up?"

"Because you changed everything."

"We can't...I've been misleading you. It's not possible. We're in business."

"You want me."

"I..."

His eyes twinkle. "It's okay. I want you too."

"It's not easy for me. I don't know why."

He narrows his eyes as he looks at me. "It started making sense to me, that you feel safer if I'm unavailable. You won't have any expectations and I won't have any of you. But see...that's not the way I envisioned you and I would go."

"There is no you and I. We've had some close calls but
—"

"There's always been a you and I. Except only you and I know it. Only you and I know all the touches that never happened. All the kisses we never took. All the damned dances I didn't dance with you."

I look away, unable to fully grasp what this all means.

We end up heading to his place, and all the time I'm telling myself I can have him. He's available, and he's looking at me like...like he's still interested.

"You son of a bitch! You lied to me," I finally say when we arrive and sit down in his living room, the truth of everything hitting me.

"I let you believe what you wanted."

"For how fucking long?"

"Two weeks. I would've told you sooner if I didn't have the eerie suspicion that you like the idea of me being taken, that you feel safer around me believing I'm not making a move on you." His eyes sparkle devilishly.

I'm shocked and already fired up by the first sentence. "Two weeks! I've been driving myself up the wall trying not to..."

He laughs and touches my ear. I feel tickles all over me.

"You think too much, and do too little," he rasps.

"You do too much and think too little of the consequences."

"What are you afraid of?"

"You. Everything blowing up in my face."

"That's not happening. But I want you blowing up in my face. Would you let me taste you, Bryn? Huh? If we went for it, would you let me finally taste you?"

"Christos."

"I've never met a woman whose scent made me want to devour her like yours does. You confuse me, Bryn. You make me want to protect you and at the same time you make me want to break you. I want you to stop thinking and just fucking feel me. Feel this."

He catches me by the back of his neck and puts his thumb on my mouth when we hear the doorbell.

His phone starts ringing, but he doesn't pick up.

A minute later, a familiar blonde arrives. Christos doesn't look up from me, his hand still on the back of my neck. "We're busy here," he says.

"Oh," Miranda says.

Seeing her here makes me panic horribly, as if I've been caught doing something wrong. "No, I was leaving." I stand and gather my things.

Aaric is on his feet. "Why?" he asks me.

I point at her, obviously. "You've got company."

"That's right. You." He nods even as I turn around. "Bryn. Stay. Hey, stay." He grabs my shoulders and turns me to face him.

"She said she was leaving," Miranda says defensively behind my back.

"Thanks, Miranda," he says flatly, not looking at her, only looking at me with what seems like panic in his eyes.

"Okay, I'm leaving, enjoy her, Christos, while she lasts," Miranda says coolly.

I hear her footsteps recede, but not even then does Aaric release his grip on my shoulders.

"Why are you leaving?" he demands, his brows low.

"She was here."

"I'm with you. We were having a good time. Why do you suppose I'd rather spend time with her than with you?" He seems vexed, his eyebrows low over his eyes, his eyes shining menacingly.

"I..."

"Why don't you hang out with me? Why always business?" He slides one of his hands up from my shoulder to slide it under the fall of my hair.

"Because we'd do well not to confuse things."

"Confuse the shit out of them."

"She's your girlfriend!"

He arches a brow.

"Your ex!"

He just stares.

"I don't want to be all hot and bothered making out with you on your couch and some woman walks in—"

"She's turning in her key once she finishes picking up her stuff." He drops his hands, sighing, and I shift on my feet as he puts his hands in his pockets and stares at me from a few feet away.

I raise my eyes. My voice wavers. "I can't do this, it's too complicated."

"Do you want this?" he asks.

"It's just that the timing…"

"There's always going to be something wrong with the timing. Or with me. Or with you. Or with some other bullshit." He clenches his jaw, his eyes brilliantly intense as he takes another step. "I'm asking if you want this, Bryn Kelly."

"Do you?" I croak.

"I want you more than you could possibly fathom."

He smells so good I feel dizzy, my brain completely out of order as I go up on tiptoes and graze his lips with mine.

I realize what I'm doing and drop back down, and when I do, I'm red head to toe. "I don't know what's come over me." I sit up and straighten myself.

"Whatever it is, I approve," he rasps huskily, his eyes smiling in pure male pleasure.

Seeing my blush intensify, he cups my face and sets his nose to mine—brilliant, lustful eyes staring into my eyes. "Hey. Don't fight it."

"I have to. I'd be stupid not to."

"Why?"

"Because. You…bother me, Aaric."

"I want you, Bryn."

I gulp and squirm in my panties.

"I still want you, little bit."

My heart is racing harder each time he repeats those words.

"I wanted you before. That doesn't hold a candle to the way I want you now." He takes my shoulders, looking at me. "I'll try to be patient. I didn't have time before, but I do now," he continues. "But you're something I've wanted for a very long time, Bryn, and I'm only human."

"Aaric, if things get messy, then we're fucked."

"They don't have to get messy as long as we're clear with each other and set some boundaries."

"Like no exclusivity? No, thanks."

"I didn't say that."

"The way you've carried on these years, I think I see more of the boy you were than there is actually left."

"You didn't want the boy."

"You don't know that," I shoot back, angry at him putting the boy down.

"I *do* know that."

"There were reasons. Mainly me. But I'd have a do-over if I could. That's how much I regret not seeing what if I'd kissed you back that day."

He clenches his jaw.

"But you...I just don't know that this can go anywhere," I say.

"It goes to my bed. You and me in it. For as long as we want to."

"Then what?" I answer myself, "Then we remain friendly. Business partners?"

"I'm never going to be your enemy, if that's what you're thinking." He strokes a hand down my hair, staring into my eyes as he adds, "I don't want to hurt you. I've never wanted to hurt you. I thought I knew what I wanted. I wanted A, but then you come back into my life. Turning things around."

"So you wanted A, what the hell am I, Z?"

He laughs. "You're the rest."

He watches me pick up my things, plunging his hands into his pockets as I head to the door and glance back at him.

"Not the start, but the end," he says.

I just smile, trying to hide the fact that my heart is skipping, and I head out for the safety of my apartment, where no tempting sex god tells me he wants me. Where the boy of my past is still a memory.

good enough

Bryn

"Don't lick my balls, man, tell me the stats," Christos tells Cole as they examine HOS market research.

A team of five other men and women are present. I've been silently watching Christos who has only been speaking to Cole throughout the meeting.

"Well, fuck, you're moody," Cole grumbles, sending the paperwork Christos's way.

Christos scans the documents while the team begins explaining to the rest of us.

Aaric watches the presentation—silent.

Something about the fact that he's so quiet seems sexy to me. He's clearly the more powerful man in the room, but his attitude is calm, in control, subdued, even though his energy is a pulsing, magnetizing, electric thing.

I exhale and try to take notes. The information we have gathered will be incorporated into the software this week. I'm trying to focus on business—exclusively, because whenever I start thinking of Aaric and the possibility of being with him, I get distracted and my childhood fears arise.

Mom once told me if you want to earn yourself half a man, be half of a woman. If you want a full man, you need to be the full version of yourself. Never expect anyone to complete you. Don't be two halves to make a whole, be two wholes and make something more.

I'm trying to be that.

But the truth is, I'm running on adrenaline here. Fantasizing about this man touching me—taking me—is thrilling, and now that I see him every day, the sexual tension between us is thick enough it's a miracle other people can fit inside this room with us.

I'm silent as they keep hashing things out, and once the group departs, Aaric gives me a look that makes me linger behind as they shut the door.

"So if the warehouse across the street is available and yours, I'd like that. It'll be the perfect place. When do you think it can be ready?"

"With money, anything can be ready fast."

"I'm so glad I partnered with you." I smile.

He reclines in his chair with a cocky smirk, his eyes gleaming ruthlessly. "Am I good enough for you now?"

"Fuck you, I don't care about your money." I shoot him a scowl.

"You care so much you've been begging me for it."

"I'm not interested in you in that way because of your money."

"Then I see no problem why you can't go out on a date with me."

"You had a fiancé only weeks ago. While you have no issues, *I* mind it."

"And yet you've never been interested in me like this before. Could the competition be whetting your appetite, sweetheart?"

"It's not whetting my anything."

"Is it wetting your thighs, love?"

"I resent you calling me endearments in that tone."

"I can't help it if they sound irreverent—you beg for it." He stands to approach.

"You know what? You really are a moody son of a bitch!" I cry, standing to leave.

He reaches out to grab my wrist, and he yanks me to his chest, and the mouth that had just been cursing me is suddenly claiming mine.

I'm shocked enough that I freeze. But he is kissing me.

Kissing me stupid.

Fucking kissing me like I've never been kissed before.

And unlike the time we were kids, he doesn't relent.

His hand slides up to grip a wad of my hair in his fist, and Aaric slants his head, exerting pressure with his mouth, forcing me to open my mouth for him. "Open, little bit," he rasps commandingly.

I do—because...I don't know.

Oh God, his tongue should be illegal! All of him should be illegal. He thrusts it into my mouth, kissing me—passion, sexual frustration, more.

And what started out as an angry, punishing kiss soon starts becoming softer, his hands begin to explore me, he begins to really savor me, to caress the back of my head with his fingers.

He lowers his head and grazes his teeth over my nipple, his hands kneading. I'm grabbing at him too, sort of out of control. I can't think of anything except how much I want this—him—how much I ache all over. How good he smells, how the calluses in his hands feel against my skin, and how his thick lips feel as he moves his mouth over my nipple.

He's panting, his breath hitting my skin as we stare at each other.

I take inventory of the situation and realize he weighs a ton, and that he's hard against my tummy.

His lips hover over mine, his forehead, his eyes, his entire face hovering over me before he leans down and takes my mouth. Softly at first, brushing his fingertips over my forehead as if I've got something he needs to brush back. But I don't. I don't think I do. Hell, I don't care if I do. I grab his shoulders and massage a little.

"Aaric," I beg, lifting my mini dress so he can touch me.

"You fucking tease," he rasps, leaning to lick his tongue into my ear. I close my eyes as he dips it into my ear and I feel a warm shiver shoot down my spine.

"You fucking tease," he says, starting to undo my buttons, and I just don't even know what to say but please undo my buttons, please make it stop, please give me take me do whatever you want but don't stop touching me.

"Do you like teasing me?" he says, opening my top, and when I nod and bite my lip nervously, he's lowering his face, sucking my nipple as if in punishment.

I groan and turn my head aside as he sucks me again, slipping his hand into my waistband and panties. "Do you like getting me hard?"

I groan, feeling him rub my clit at the same time he grinds his erection against me.

"You're so much more trouble than you look."

I feel his hard bulge bite into my pelvis as he shifts, raising my legs to his sides. I raise my arms and curl them around his neck as he settles himself between my thighs, and before I know it he's free of his slacks, pushing them down to his ankles, and he's sheathed and he's entering me, so huge I almost scream from the sensation of fullness, and then I just want more, more, *more*, and he's giving me so much we're both just bodies moving and straining to get closer.

We're groaning, kissing and groping, my back nearly breaking against the desk and my nails nearly drawing his blood on his back, and his hips relentlessly pummeling against mine as we kiss like our lives depend on it and like we have no control, like we're animals and don't care of the consequences, only want to fuck and taste, fuck and groan, fuck and bite down on each other's tongue and then suck it and kiss while our breaths explode against one another's face and our bodies strain to get closer and our hips madly hump and we're humping like crazy and I'm crying out and he's coming and we're both coming and it's coming over us like crazy and it's here between us and even then we keep fucking as we come...even keep fucking a little slower as it starts easing—

--what's my name?

--fuck, he weighs a ton

--shit, but I'm not saying a peep about that because I still want his dick inside me for a little longer

--God. BEST SEX EVER!

--shit. What did I do?

--um, this is going to be awkward.

It's actually not awkward yet because he pulls out, and he's still hard, and he rolls me around, makes me wet again, and gives it to me again.

There, folded over.

We don't talk, it would ruin it, but our bodies do the talking for us, his hands, his sucking mouth, his groans and my moans, the way we move, sort of like our bodies don't agree with the words we sometimes tell each other, like being close is what we were born to do—how we instinctively crave to be.

When he asks me to come, come harder for him, I come a second time, and it feels like I do come harder. Harder because he wanted me to.

He's breathing harshly in my ear moments later, and I'm fighting to breathe at all.

I really think we needed that. It was a good way to work each other out of our systems. He stands and helps me up, and then he helps me rearrange my clothes.

He looks at me and there's intimacy there and heat. I look down.

"That was actually the best sex I've ever had," I breathe as he steps aside and heads over to his window.

He drags a hand over his jaw, staring outside, his shoulders broad and square.

"God, you're an asshole."

I start to leave. He stops me, a hand on my elbow. "Come home with me tonight."

"What for?"

"For more of that."

I exhale. "So you liked it too."

He looks at my mouth.

The look melts me, heats me, it's so raw. I breathe, "You're an asshole. I'm not going anywhere with you until you admit it." I tilt my chin, but inside I really just crave to hear it. Our eyes hold deadlocked.

"Put your hand on the front of my pants."

"What?"

"Do it."

I do. He's really hard. I rub him. "Did you not come?" A smile curves my lips. I'm teasing him.

He looks at me, the heat intensifying.

"Oh my God, you've got pre-cum coming out already..."

And when I gasp he moves swiftly to take my mouth and kiss me stupid. Long and slow.

"I can wrap up at seven. Why don't you meet me in the lobby when I'm done?"

He halts my hand, on his hard dick, and doesn't remove it. I can feel him, hard and pulsing as I try to swallow. "I have a date with Natchez. One of my dogs. But can I use a computer while you finish off..."

"Use my laptop."

I pry my hand away from his hot body and grab his laptop, then I start to take it outside.

"You can stay here if you'd like."

I halt midtrack. Eye the leather sectional in the seating area of his office and the glass coffee table before it. "This will do." I smile, and he smiles briefly before he heads behind his desk to get business done.

On his laptop, I discover a folder titled **Bryn**. I click on it. Pictures of me appear. Some when I was younger, others of me now.

I look down at my lap. He's moody today, but a part of me knows I've been giving him a tough time about us. About me and him. I can't imagine how frustrating I have been, and how hard it is for him to see me every day too, and maybe want things that I keep fighting him on.

As Aaric finishes up, I close his laptop and bring it back to his desk.

"You have a folder called Bryn in your computer." I feel flushed, and I'm as unable to stop the flush as I am to keep from smiling. "I have one too but in my mind. Called Aaric."

He looks up at me, eyebrows high.

"I've got two what ifs in my life that have always hurt me to think about. You're one of them, Aaric," I admit.

He stands up and pushes his chair in, coming around to lean on his desk, attentive. "What's the other one?"

I hesitate.

"The night my parents died, they called me, I got home around midnight. Got ready for bed. At 12:55 a.m., I thought about calling back, but I convinced myself it would be better if I called the next day."

"12:59 is the time the fire started," he says.

I nod, my throat suddenly tight.

His eyes shadow, and for a while he says nothing.

"When Leilani went into labor, I was away on business. She ended up in some shitty hospital. My daughter didn't make it." He eyes me for a long moment. "I thought I didn't want her. I convinced myself it happened because I didn't want her."

"Of course it didn't happen because of that. She wasn't in your plans. We couldn't have known."

"We should've."

"But we didn't."

He reaches out to touch my shoulder, peering at my face. "Hey. The fire wasn't your fault."

"Neither is the death of your baby."

He looks at my whole face, then at my mouth. "Some what ifs, some you never get to do over, Bryn," he says.

I blink, dipping my head in consent. "Sometimes you get another try," I breathe.

As I hold back my tears, he sets his thumb on my bottom lip, and kisses me. It's just a soft kiss as he says, "I'll take you home."

And I ask if he can take me to Natchez instead, just because I want to prolong this. Just because, even when consciously I want to put distance between us, subconsciously I seem to want something else.

in the stars

Bryn

I can't sleep. I can't eat. This is more. This is more than I ever thought possible. *Him*—how much I want him. How much I care. I toss and turn all night, thinking of nothing but Christos and how much I want to do the brave thing, and for once in my life let myself fall without worrying. Let myself fall for him—the guy I've been falling for since I was seventeen.

I've always been reliable and levelheaded. Cautious, you could say. But that bitch is gone. That was the young me. The adult me says yes, go for it, you have been into this guy since the moment you saw him, greasy and hot at the shop. I want to try and see where this goes, but I'm scared it will end up provoking my heart, even while up on the highest shelf where I'd put it. But who am I kidding? It's no longer on my shelf, it's been in his. For a long time.

On Saturday morning, I look up my horoscope for the weekend.

DEAR CAPPIE,

THE STARS ARE ALIGNING FOR YOU! IF YOU'VE HAD YOUR HOPES ON A CERTAIN SOMEONE, THIS WEEK MIGHT BE THE TIME YOU TWO CAN TAKE THE RELATIONSHIP TO THE NEXT LEVEL. JUST BE PATIENT, AS THEY SAY, ROME WASN'T BUILT IN A DAY...

I'm not sure how I feel about this. It says nothing about what happens if you jump recklessly into a forbidden romance.

No, I am totally not the Cappie that horoscope is talking about. But once Becka told me your sun sign is not the only clue as to the weather around you. She had used a handy little internet tool to find out my ascendant, based on the hour you were born. So I read Pisces next.

DEAR PISCES,

BOY YOU MUST BE THRILLED THE SQUARE ALIGNMENT HAS EASED SOME THIS MONTH, AND WITH MARS BACK IN GOOD FORM AFTER ITS RETROGRADE IN YOUR HOUSE OF TRAVEL, YOU SHOULD BE READY FOR BUSINESS AND PLEASURE, BOTH! KEEP YOUR EYE ON YOUR GOALS AND DON'T FORGET TO HAVE A LIT-TLE FUN THIS AUGUST WHILE VENUS TRAVELS YOUR FIFTH HOUSE OF LOVE AND CREATIVITY.

"I do enjoy reading these suckers, though I never pay attention to any negative things they have to say. I only run with the good ones. This time though, it's way off." I sigh.

"Read mine. Wait, *you* read it first before telling me what it says. Shit, don't tell me if it's bad."

"What's your sign?"

"Taurus. Ruled by Venus, I apparently like very beautiful and expensive things." Sara smirks while taking a peek. "What does it say?"

"Don't peek and don't talk, I can't concentrate reading with noise around!" I start reading hers.

DEAR TAURUS,

AFTER THE RECENT MERCURY RETROGRADE IN YOUR SISTER SIGN VIRGO DURING THE MONTH OF JULY, YOU'RE BACK IN FULL FORM AND ABLE TO WORK OFF THE KINKS IN YOUR COMMUNICATIONS. NOW IS THE TIME TO IRON OUT THE DETAILS OF THAT PROFESSIONAL PLAN YOU'VE BEEN HOLDING IN THE BACK BURNER, AND IF A RELATIONSHIP HAS FELT THE ROUGH AND TUMBLE OF THE STARS, REMEMBER THE UNIVERSE ALWAYS HELPS US WITH COURSE CORRECTIONS TO FIX WHAT'S BROKEN, OR LEARN TO LET GO.

"What does it say?"

"Dear Taurus," I begin. "If you still love him, go for it. Don't wait for my astrologer permission, don't wait for me to give you a safety net, just do it!"

"What?" She starts reading and says, "Bryn, you are a lousy astrologer. You'd die poor."

I can't seem to fully stop a giggle as I set it aside. "No, really. You're hooked on him, Sara. I do think you need to find him. Why wait? You can be waiting forever. Why do we give our power away?" I frown. "I mean, we're bombarded by all these marketers telling us what to think, how to feel about ourselves, we wait to see what others think about our clothes to determine if we really like them. We wait for an astrologer to tell us the coast is clear to do something we've been wanting to do. It's wrong."

I chew my nail. My mind wanders back to Christos and I wonder why I had the balls to give Sara this advice when I don't have any balls of my own, apparently.

I also remember touching Christos's balls and how much I wanted to go down on him. A pang of unwelcome little feelings strike and I'm not really sure if I'll be able to push them away, but I try to, especially considering I was talking to Sara about her love life. Not mine.

"Let's do something we really want to do. Let's finally do something for ourselves, take our own advice."

"Okay then." She makes a phone call. "Hi, I'd like to see if you can do me a favor and check back on the guest list for last year. I need the name of someone." Her eyes spark up as if the answer delights her. "Really? You'd do that for me? Thank you!" She hangs up. "He's helping me find him. Your turn."

"Did you really call?" I ask, doubting that she did.

"Do you want to call back to verify? Come on. Your turn. Go after him, Bryn."

I bite down on my lip for a moment, then I grab my phone and decide that I don't want to keep wondering *what if* anymore. Not when there's something I can do about it.

So I've been thinking about it.

And I've decided this is healthy, this is the best scenario possible, neither of us expects more.

So please tell Christos that it's yes.

Tell Bit for me
I do want more
And she won't regret it.

But let's keep it low key please. I don't want anyone at Christos and Co or your brother to know

I don't report to my employees or my brother, but I understand your concern. I'll be discreet as long as you want to keep a lid on it.

I read the message, relieved, when suddenly a new one pops up.

What are you wearing now?

I tingle.

Panties and a T-shirt.

What color panties?

Soft lilac.

Soft lilac. What material are they?

They're silky. A little sheer.

And under the T-shirt?

Nothing.

What color T-shirt?

I close my eyes.

I just took it off.

Butterflies in my stomach as I read his reply.

Take off the rest.
Put on one of your little dresses
And meet me downstairs in 20 minutes.

I reach for my panties. *Bryn, what the hell are you doing?*
Honestly, something has just clicked in my mind. The fact that I no longer care. I want him—desperately. And for a long time, Christos has wanted *me*. I don't want to deny myself his presence, his laughter, his touch. Fuck what the cosmos says, or if it's written in the stars, or if its doomed, or if it's right or not. Life goes by in a blink, and I don't want to blink one second and once again, find him gone.

We walk along Gramercy Park until it starts to rain. One second we're dry, the next we're getting pounded by raindrops. Christos glances around and motions farther down the block, to a tall skyscraper. "Over there."

He rushes me to a building where the doorman greets him.

"Penthouse still empty?" He runs his hand through his wet hair as I feel water drip down my legs.

"Sir, yes. They're putting in the finishing touches until they start showing next month."

"We need shelter for a moment," he says with a smirk.

The doorman pulls out a double set of keys. "Of course, sir, go right in. I'll be sure you're not disturbed."

He slides a key into the elevator slot, then uses the second one to open the double doors when we reach the top floor.

We walk into a huge, vacant marble-floored penthouse.

"You own this?"

"Yes."

"The penthouse or the building?" I gaze out at the panoramic views.

Silence.

I turn. "Wow. You amaze me."

"*You're* amazing," he husks back. He walks forward. "Did you take off what I told you?"

"Yes." Flushing, I motion to him. "Seems right that you take off something too. It's only fair."

"Life isn't fair."

He smiles, but when he stares at me for a moment, something flickers in his eyes. He starts to unbutton his wet, white shirt, then he shrugs it off his powerful shoulders.

"Are we even?"

I gulp. "Not even close," I breathe and hold his wicked— w i c k e d—gaze. His tattoo is shining wetly on his shoulder and bicep, and I get wet in places the sunlight doesn't touch.

His chest is wet. I try not to notice.

But I notice.

Oh boy.

He is speaking to me.

Did he ask me something?

I can't hear. A drop of water slides down his abs and falls into his belly button.

His pecs are hard, his muscles so defined I could trace them with a pencil. My tongue could act as a pencil, I suppose.

I want to trace the tattoo with my fingers, his whole body with my fingers.

I lick my lips and he is watching me, speculatively.

I take a step, then a few quicker ones, and then I'm pressing my mouth to his nipple. I lick the drop.

He groans.

A low, pained sound as his hand comes to cup the back of my head.

I bend and lick the other drop, close to his belly button, on his strong, ripped abs, and my tongue dips into his belly button even though there's not a drop there. When I place my hands on his abs, they feel so hard. They constrict beneath my fingers, and I kiss him on each square. My heart pounds as he holds the back of my head, one hand on my skull, the other curving possessively around my neck—exerting the slightest pressure to keep my face where it is. With my lips on his warm, wet skin. I ease up and meet his gaze.

He pulls me up higher with his hand, looking straight at me with devastatingly tender eyes. His jaw starts working, his lips pressing into a grim line. He fists my hair, starts pulling me up. I go willingly.

Pressing my mouth between his pecs. Then as he pulls me up another inch, he dives down, and the wet raindrops are replaced by his wet mouth.

Something overtakes us. My hands on his wet shoulders, twining first and then gripping the wet muscle, nails in his back as his arms go around me and my legs go around *him* as he devours my mouth.

Christos grabs my ass and boosts me.

Up higher, so I'm almost higher than he is. I'm canting down my head so he can ravage me and massage my butt. His beautiful erection is almost a table for me to sit on. I feel so tiny even when he has me lifted higher, as if I were a little girl and he wanted to show me the world.

"Aaric," I breathe. My own driving desire shocks me.

He turns me up against the wall, our mouths fused as he jams a hand between our bodies and touches me there.

I'm not wearing any panties—only his slacks separate us, and as he kisses me and strokes his fingers along my wetness, I groan.

He groans too, more undone than I am.

He tears free and hunches down, and he nuzzles my stomach over my dress.

My breath snags in my throat when he rasps something unintelligible, nudging my dress upward with his nose—then his breath is on the skin beneath my belly button.

His fingertips run up the back of my knee, his nose pressing into my abdomen. He smells my skin.

I whimper, my whole body tightening in yearning.

He flicks his tongue out to lick my abs, a wet circle around my belly button, and he groans, as if my taste is addictive.

I'm melting.

His hand continues trailing up the back of my thigh, leisurely shifting to my inner thigh, under my skirt.

His eyes shine as he looks up at me. But that look changes when he touches my sex with the tip of his index finger.

The damp spot is unmistakable.

He clenches his jaw. His gaze? It's not playful anymore; it's raw and ridiculously primitive. He tugs the fabric aside.

"You've thought of this. Me kissing you here."

"No."

"You want this."

"No…"

He moves his finger over my sex. "This tells me yes."

He ducks his head and presses his warm tongue and slowly runs it over my sex, tasting me.

I shudder from the shock of the warm flick of his tongue over my wet spot, this time a little slower, a little firmer.

My knees try to snap closed, but he grabs me by the thighs and holds me in place as he kisses me more, angling his head to taste more of me. Lick more of me. Twirl his tongue and caress more of me. "You're beautiful, Bryn. You taste so good, little bit."

He spreads me a little farther open, his big body hunched between my legs, his shoulders bunched up as he keeps his head between my legs. He's toying with my sex lips. I feel his hand coming to cup my sex with so much tenderness that it hurts my heart. He inserts two fingers inside me as he cups one breast with his hand and raises his head to look up at me.

My breasts are moving up and down with my harsh breaths. Almost begging for his attention, one of them covered by his palm. The other so lonely and puckered it hurts.

I bite my lower lip discreetly, my eyes meeting his for a fraction of a second—and I'm able to see the total pleasure in his eyes of seeing me undone like this, completely helpless. I want to have the energy to pull him closer, to ravage this man, but I can't move one whit, because I'm undone seeing him like this too. Along with the pleasure in his eyes, I see heat—heat that this is doing shit to him, that he's thought of this too.

He stands back over me, leans over, and brushes his lips over mine, and I groan and feel myself go lax beneath him as he slides two fingers between my legs, all while kissing me—slow and thorough—his other hand tweaking my nipple in a move that I'd assume should be a little painful but is actually so pleasurable I arch and gasp, my gasp only inviting his tongue to keep working me into a frenzy. He roams his tongue in my mouth as his fingers move, one inch, two inches, three, four...in and out, slowly, priming me.

My hands grip his hard shoulders. My legs twine around his hips, even as he remains dressed from the waist down.

I start to kiss him back with all the passion I kept hidden for so many years. This man kissing me is the only man who makes me nervous. Makes me babble. Makes me afraid. Makes me excited. Makes me *want.*

There are the kinds of things that you don't choose—they just happen, sometimes with people you don't want to react to as fiercely as you do. Christos has always been mine. My *what if*, and also my *why him.*

Right now he's the center of my universe. His nearness all I know. And that gold sea of desire in his eyes as he tears free to look down at me questioningly, as if he can't believe I'm so fucking hungry. It's the fucking hottest thing I've ever seen in a man.

He grabs my dress and pulls it over my head.

Groaning, out of control, I duck my head and nuzzle my nose as he rains kisses on my stomach.

They're not sweet kisses, not really. They have so much tongue and teeth: nips, gentle bites, hungry licks.

"Aaric, I want to see you too," I groan.

He shushes me by nudging my legs farther apart and looking straight at me. Looking at me *there*. At the tingly, aching spot he just kissed with wicked intimacy. His eyes cool and assessing and at the same time hot and reverent.

He presses a simple kiss to my curls.

I buck from the pleasure, and he leans forward again and flicks his warm, slow, lovely tongue out to taste me again.

Colors begin dancing behind my eyelids.

I tense up as an orgasm starts building, surprising me.

He stands then, and takes my arms and lays them against the wall, rocking his clothed hips against my naked body, his hard cock, covered only by his slacks, against my bare sex.

All while he lowers and gives my mouth the biggest fucking of its life.

I go off the next instant with a soft cry, Christos rocking against me as I do, his mouth and hands and strength all I know as he growls and comes with me, the dampness seeping from his pants and against my wet sex.

As the waves start dissipating, I become aware of how we stand—me naked, him just shirtless and tattooed, his slacks damp from the rain, my hair tangled, my whole body still shuddering in aftershocks.

I laugh, and his laugh is rich and deep as he chuckles too, brushing my hair back with one hand.

He drives me home and walks me to my door. Sara's in the kitchen and obviously catches on quickly enough when she sees him.

"You're welcome to stay, Christos," Sara tells him as we walk into the living area.

"He was on his way out. My boss has a big dick. I mean, my boss is an absolute dick. I need my rest."

Sara's eyes widen, Christos just laughs.

He leans over. "I'm not your boss, but when you need someone to boss you in bed—call me." He winks.

"You're right, you're my business partner. You offered up the dough."

"Maybe you should offer me a nightcap."

"Christos, come on, my roommate is here…"

"To my disadvantage," he agrees, his eyes darkening. "Goodnight, bit."

"Goodnight, Aaric."

The door shuts, and I raise my hand to Sara. "Don't ask."

"I have to!" she complains as she follows me to my room. "Are you two…?"

I throw myself down on my bed. "You dared me to go after what I wanted."

"So?"

"So I am," I say, giddy as I hug my pillow and laugh. "Sara, I can't even deal with myself right now," I groan, flipping to my back and staring up at the ceiling, seeing his face as

I came for him, his face as he came *in his pants* with me. The sexiest expression imaginable on his sexy-as-fuck face.

fifth ave

Bryn

We're testing the software in the basement of the office warehouse. I pull my chair closer to the desk and keep my eyes on the computer screen as the developer clicks a few commands on the keyboard.

We wait.

And there it is, the House of Sass software loads and opens to the home screen.

The logo looks gorgeous, in a sleek, simple font and a subtle gray color. The background is white and modern, with just a tiny bit of violet shade in both *O*'s of the name.

The navigator looks easy to access, and they've already uploaded a sample "closet" outfit for me to see.

As I take it all in, I'm not aware that I cover my mouth. I can't breathe from the disbelief of seeing my plan—something that only existed in my mind—becoming alive right before my eyes.

Aaric leans against a desk behind us and watches, then he steps forward and peers over my shoulder. His gaze ruthlessly scans the computer screen. "Do that again," he tells the developer.

The tech guy reloads the app.

I want to cry from the excitement.

"Too slow," he says. "The second I click, I want it uploaded. No wait."

He takes me by the elbow and lifts me to my feet as we prepare to head back upstairs.

"App version coming along?" he asks the developer.

"We have an app?" I ask, surprised.

Christos looks at me with a glint of amusement in his eye. "Yes, bit. We will have an app."

"Of course," I say, "of course we will have an app," covering my surprise and acting cool in front of the developer but smiling happily at Christos.

As we exit the basement area, I try to keep up with his long strides as we head up the stairs. "Christos, I'm thinking. We can place sponsor ads discreetly on the free version. Or people can pay for the full version. Every sale sends underprivileged child clothes, food, and books."

He raises his brows.

"Because people need it. Just like people need this software in their lives," I add.

We reach the second-floor landing, and he faces me with an approving smile. He studies my face for a moment. "Are you busy later?"

"I hoped to work."

"Would you consider working while having dinner with me?"

"That would totally not be work."

He takes my chin and turns my head around. "Have dinner with me."

I swallow, admitting, "I'd like that very much."

We take a black car and head from Brooklyn to Manhattan. It's rush hour, but we make it in fifty minutes.

I usually travel by subway, so seeing New York as the sun sets while I ride in the back of the car with him makes me breathless. Growing up, I always wanted to experience New York. And now I share an apartment here with Sara, and this big city feels like home—at last.

And beside me is Aaric, the boy from my past who's no longer just a boy, and no longer just in my past. He's very much a man, very much in my present. My heart is thumping in excitement as a hot little tingle between my thighs grows at his nearness and because he's got his hand on my thigh, lounging in his seat as if his hand belongs there.

I like the way it feels too much to do that.

It excites me, true, that he's a little forward. He's more brazen now, as a man, I think because he also knows that I'm no longer a girl. I'm a woman, and I can take more. He can push…just a little more.

I swallow in anticipation.

We reach his brownstone, and he leads me up to the top floor, then opens the doors that lead to the balcony. I'm speechless by the view of the park spreading out before us, the shadows of sunset streaking across the tops of the trees.

"This is incredible," I say, laughing in delight as I drink up the most vibrant city in the United States and possibly, the world.

Christos is smiling when I turn. He's got his hands inside his pockets, a look of thoughtful warmth on his face.

"I really like the combination of traditional and contemporary of your brownstone. It's kind of like you."

"I'm traditional?"

"Part of you. Your desire for a family and stability. But another part of you is cutting edge. The business side."

"Glad you've discovered those two sides of me. There's yet a third." He begins prowling forward.

"What third."

"An animalistic, crazy as hell, third side of me that you should run away from."

"Me or everyone?"

"Just you. Because you're the one who brings it about." He winks, then brings me forward and laughs when I blush. He brushes my lips against his.

"Are you hungry?" he asks.

"Starved."

"Get changed for dinner then, and we'll head off."

"This is all I have to wear."

"No, bit." He shakes his head. "It's not."

He lets his eyes drift past my shoulders to one of the doors. Confused, I walk into a small bedroom and am surprised to see a silver box waiting on the bed.

There's a card that reads, **bit** on it. I open the box and pull out a dress.

Oh my God!

It's not just a dress. It's a dress from MY LINE. The first dress made for House of Sass.

I'm trembling from the excitement as I slip it on, zip it up, and hurry to the full-length mirror.

The shock of seeing myself wearing my own high-end-made design freezes me on the spot.

My eyes run down my curves, taking in how slinky the material is, how sexy and elegant the cut is. He had it done in the most decadent violet shade ever. I blink several times and walk slowly toward my reflection, putting my fingers on the mirror just to be sure I'm awake.

Is this really my life? I feel like a royal princess. I've never been pampered by a guy. I've never been seriously wined and dined either. To go out with Aaric tonight feels surreal.

I step outside, and the feeling only intensifies when I spot him. He's wearing slacks and a white shirt, with the top buttons unbuttoned. Freshly showered and gorgeous. His eyes leisurely tracking my frame.

"I love this," I say, glancing sheepishly down at my dress. "Do you?"

His eyes twinkle. "That's putting it mildly. You look stunning in it." He eyes me appreciatively.

"Thank you. I'm feeling high on emotions, so forgive me if I tear up."

I wave my face with my hand and he approaches. "You're welcome. You deserve it after what I put you through."

"Your awful vetting, you mean?"

He nods, sliding a hand down my waist, then brushing my hair back as he drinks in my every feature with lazy interest.

We smile at each other. He then grabs his keys and cell phone from a foyer table, leaning over me to do it. My breath catches when his hot whisper trickles along my ear. "You have no clue how much I look forward to taking that off you tonight," he whispers and sets a kiss on my cheek.

"I just put it on!" At his answering chuckle, I try to suppress a giggle, but he leans over and takes it with his lips, kissing me softly, pressing me into him with his hands splayed on my back.

I can feel his erection against my abdomen, and the memory of what it feels like inside of me makes me whimper as his tongue moves over mine. I sink into him, time and space evaporating to nothing as I kiss him back.

He tears free with effort.

"Let's go," he says, his fingers touching the small of my back as he leads me out of his place and to the elevators.

Christos is watching me over the fancy red menu. We smile.

My feelings toward him are becoming more and more intense.

I know he's had rosters of women; why he'd want to involve himself with me is a mystery. But he doesn't even try to hide the desire in his eyes. And even more confusing is why I'd want to get myself involved with him, of all the guys? He's the one that is the most difficult to understand, and impossible to control, plus why ruin a possibly good business relationship? Why ruin what could be a very healthy friendship-slash-business relationship?

Because he's adorable when he smiles and his eyes shine a little brighter—a little more green than gold.

And when he looks at me, sometimes, as if he's still the boy that had a crush on me, I melt. I've missed this guy.

At the end of the evening, accused of eating most of his dessert and mine, I laugh and snuggle close as he helps me out of my chair, and there's nowhere else I'd rather be.

After dinner, we walk down 5th Avenue—it's one of those rare walks where you're just walking for pleasure, without any rush of having to be anywhere or wanting to be any other place than where you are.

"I've never really opened up to a guy before—about my parents. It's so easy with you. I've been scared that you could hurt me. But lately I've been thinking that I don't want to be scared anymore. That if anything, you're the one guy I'd trust not to hurt me."

I reach out and slip my hand into his—then realize what I'm doing.

"I can't believe I did that." I'm so shocked by how naturally I grabbed his hand that I try to withdraw my hand.

"Why." He gives me a gentle squeeze, keeping my grip in his.

"It was just so impulsive, I just..."

"Just what...." He drags his thumb over mine, his smile fading a little, his golden eyes both penetrating and coaxing.

He trails his thumb into my palm as he waits for my reply.

A million sparks rush up my arms and back.

I feel so awake when I'm close to him and also so completely uneven. It's as if he literally rocks my world, and it's hard to find my footing when he's near.

He's staring at me again, so I tuck my hand away and nervously bite on my lip.

Christos is a shark for business but he's a shark for everything he does as well. He has so much more mileage than me, even in relationships. I've never had a real one before.

It seems so easy for him to reach out and take my hand in his again, squeeze me tight.

My heart feels like it grows about ten sizes in my chest as I let the feeling sink in, let myself enjoy it.

There's a reward in simple things like letting him hold my hand, here in New York, where so many other people walk past us, unaware of this being the first time I do this. The only guy that's ever made me want to be with someone. With him.

"Christos, I want you to know that...I'm not playing games here. I know it may seem like that because I've been scared, but I'm not interested in some fling."

"I'm not planning on this being a fling. I'm dead serious about you, Bryn." He looks at me soberly, and I swallow with emotion and nod, relieved that he feels like this.

"So no other man for you? Ever?"

"No. I mean I dated for some time, but nothing serious. Not really."

"I can't believe all those idiots let you slip by."

I laugh. "There's not many of them, really. I know I seem extroverted but I'm more introvert, I'm drained around too many people. I used to think I'd be more extroverted when I grew up, but I find the opposite is actually true." I glance at his thoughtful profile. "What about you, do you find you're more open to friendships as you get older?" I say.

He shrugs. "Not really," he finally says. "There are friends, then there are acquaintances. I can count the former with the fingers of one hand." He shoots me a smile.

The wind blows through his sexy hair. I'm acutely aware of every inch of his body walking next to mine. Of everything about him. It's never been like this for me, ever. It shouldn't be like this with him, and not now. But it is; and it's difficult to put a name to the things he makes me feel.

We continue walking. Talking.

"I'm not the kind of guy that trusts people easily. I keep my circle tight and to only a few."

"And Cole?"

"I suppose Cole is more open to socializing. He wasn't the one who took care of our mother as closely. When she passed, in a way my being the eldest made me feel responsible for not only myself, but for him too."

"His father figure, so to speak."

"Yeah, well. Without a dad for your whole life, someone needs to step into the role."

I eye him. "Do you miss her? Your mom?"

"I do. But I'd seen her suffer long enough that I know she's in a better place now."

We fall silent for a while.

"I was obsessed with death in my college days," I tell him.

"Why?" He seems shocked.

"Because of my parents...when they left on their trip, I never expected I'd be saying goodbye for the last time. Then I get a call from my Aunt Cecile, and she was crying so hard, she could hardly speak." I trail off and Christos's eyes shadow.

"I'm sorry," he says.

"I'm sorry too." I swallow. "Did I ever thank you for the flowers?"

"Thank me later," he says wickedly.

"Come on, you're so not getting laid because of flowers."

His eyes darken. He shoots me a look.

"You're getting laid for other reasons," I add, tongue-in-cheek.

He slips his hand into my waistband and caresses the skin on the back of my spine.

"I was pretty fucked up for the next few months," I admit. "I kept thinking my time was coming too. I kept waiting for it to happen. It was only when I turned 21 that I finally felt like I should do something with my life and stop waiting. Because it might be a long time coming." I laugh, but sober up to add, "My Aunt Cecile died shortly after. It was hard not to fall back into my grief."

He studies me with a small smile. "So are you a hypochondriac or what?"

"No! I mean. No. It just hits you hard." I lean back and sigh. "I read this book, *Remembrance*, by Jude Deveraux, about reincarnation and how we come back over and over and find our loved ones again, so I felt better about that. Like when I met you in high school. I would bet anything that I knew you before in another life."

"Who was I?"

I smile shyly, feeling his amused gaze on my profile and somehow in my heart. "Someone crucial."

"What? Like your brother?"

"No! You know what." I snicker.

He smiles seductively, stares straight ahead, then at me. "I think knowing all this ends makes it even better, makes every moment count more. Right now this second," he snaps his finger, "just gone."

"Way to kill my enjoyment right now, Christos!"

He drapes his arm around me and we walk, laughing.

It seems natural that I press into his embrace, my whole body craving his body heat.

"Tell me something about you," I say.

"What do you want to know?"

"How you came to New York."

"I don't know. I suppose it made sense. I was making millions, and I wanted to exponentially grow. I played with stocks, and real estate was big for me. There's no more expensive real estate in the country than Manhattan. Might as well do something before I die," he teases me.

I frown and slap his arm playfully. "You're not nice."

"I've never been nice. Isn't that why you never went for me, bit?"

Flushing the color of sundried tomatoes, I look away and change the subject. "I was afraid you were...well, someone crucial," I say, and his eyes are laughing as he stares down at me.

"I don't regret that I waited," I blurt out.

"You can't mean that."

"I do. Otherwise all this...I'd be missing out on all this. Tonight."

"You're enjoying tonight?"

"You have no idea," I admit, sliding my hand up his wrist and then back down, into his.

"I'm sorry about your mom. I can tell you still miss her. It makes me want to...hug you."

"Huh?" he asks, puzzled about what I mean.

Impulsively, I reach out, and Christos lets me press his face to my chest and envelop him in a hug. He turns his head, between my breasts, and leaves it there, shaking. Oh God, is he crying? I peer down. He's laughing.

The bastard is *laughing*.

"I can get used to this," he mumbles, sliding his hands around my waist.

"You pervert. I'm trying to give you the hug I wanted to give you every time I thought of your mom sick and dying and you taking care of her, juggling school and a job, all at once."

We're smiling when we straighten.

"It's okay. I mean, it hurts, but it's okay." He stops smiling and his eyes are a little shadowed and tender as he looks down at me. "You're sweet. Smart, funny. Unique. I think the one who needs a hug is you."

"Why?"

"You're like a four-year-old, *why*? Because I say so?" he smirks.

He grabs me by the back of the neck and pulls me into his arms. Seriously, being enveloped by these thick arms feels too good.

I love how playful he is being with me right now. How easy it is to talk to him. To tell him things.

We head to his apartment with his hand still on the back of my neck, pressing me to his side. I'm warm all over by the time we head inside and grab wine and snacks.

"So when did you get the idea for House of Sass?" he asks.

"I don't know." I shrug. I settle down on one of the couches while he drops a few inches away on the same couch and pours wine for us. "I guess a few years after my parents died, after my Aunt Cecile died, and I dropped out of college. I'm drawn to things you can physically touch. I didn't consider getting into the tech side of the business until you asked me to make it bigger."

He hands me a glass of wine. "Tech has been big for years, and I see it continuing to be."

"I really like the fact that we'll have both—a physical store but a virtual advisor. I suppose I was anti-tech for a time simply because I read a study which predicted that, in our future, many of our experiences would be virtual, and what's the fun in that? I mean, a virtual kiss is not like a real one, you're kissing *air*."

"That'd be a business I'd go for, a virtual experience where you can smell the person you love, touch them, or at least trick your brain into thinking you're with them."

"But you aren't and you will always *know* that you aren't," I contradict.

He sets down his wine glass. I can tell by the mischievous gleam and the challenging lift of his eyebrow he sends my way that he's up to something. He lifts the lid of a small ivory-encrusted box on the coffee table, and extracts something silver. "Let's try it out. Close your eyes."

"What?"

He waits—obviously expecting me to hop to do his bidding. I'm tempted to ignore him, except there's that glint in his eye of pure mischief and I want to know what is causing it. So I close my eyes, smiling, and feel the barest brush over my cheeks. "Am I touching you or not?" he rasps.

"What?" The flutters in my heart caused by the touch on my cheek is proving too distracting.

"Is this my touch, or is it the tip of this pen?" he asks again.

I inhale, keeping my eyes shut as I concentrate on the feeling. His scent is too close; I can't concentrate really. He smells like my high school years, like my most secret wishes, and like a dream. Inhaling one good whiff, I exhale it reluctantly. "It's your finger," I finally say.

"Why do you say that?"

"Because!" I cry in exasperation. "You're the selfish, possessive type, you wouldn't give a pen the pleasure of doing something you want to do."

Amusement laces his voice as I try to open my eyes, and he runs the tips of two fingers over my eyelids to urge them back shut. Close to my ear, he says, "Newsflash, little bit. The pen has no feelings or pleasure, whereas *I* do, I'll give you that. Which finger?"

"I don't know. Don't mindfuck me." I exhale exasperatedly, my eyes still closed as I try to concentrate on the feeling. "It's your pinky."

"Are you sure?"

"Yes."

"Positive?"

"Yes. Wait...it's your middle finger."

"Open your eyes."

I look down and spot his pinky, then feel my stomach burn with wanting him to keep touching me, and to hide my reaction, I laugh.

"Your instinct was spot on," he says.

"Then I blew it. Now me." I reach out for the pen. "Okay, so close your eyes."

He does.

I look at him, trying to determine where to touch him and with what. I pause and just look at him. I can't take the heavy feeling I get in my chest, like there's a giant pressing his foot on my ribcage.

God, he's so gorgeous. I'm just having the time of my life with him tonight. It was always easy to talk to him, I always craved his company, but it was hard to endure it without feeling all these same things I'm feeling now.

I'm older now, a little less scared of them, a little more curious about them to fear leaping in...so here I am, gazing at his chiseled face, his strong features, his nose, his forehead, and his full plump lips, and even the blond tips of his eyelashes resting against his cheekbones.

I lean over, and press my thumb to his lips—like he did once—and then I press my lips to my thumb and ease my thumb downward so that my lips are touching, intimately pressing, against his full, perfect mouth.

So yeah, I kiss him—a peck on his mouth, feeling happy, carefree, light.

Maybe high on the enjoyable evening.

As I ease back, he opens his eyes. So do I.

He clenches his jaw, cups my face, and opens my mouth, tilting my head to kiss me harder.

"I need to pee," I say, and I giggle-groan when I realize I said that out loud.

I leap to my feet in my urgency.

He chuckles and shakes his head, his eyes raking me, head to toe.

I head into the guest bedroom, do my thing, then I step out to the large sink area and wash my hands. My gaze is trapped by the view outside the bedroom. I feel him approach like a tension pulling at my belly.

"Come to bed, bit," he whispers in my ear as he drapes the shoulder of my dress an inch down my arm. "My bed," he specifies, kissing the round curve of my shoulder.

He turns me to face him with one hand, and I'm breathless when I see the look in his eyes as he leads me there.

He releases me inside his bedroom, walks to pull the curtains closed, then slowly turns to watch me stand in the middle of the room. I'm so nervous and yet so eager I can't breathe right.

"Come here."

I do, because he asks and because I want to, very much.

He pulls me close.

"You're driving me crazy, you know," he says, his voice so sexy and husky.

"I know. You do the same to me. You're a mirror."

"Am I? Can you see how gorgeous you are to me in the way I look at you, huh?"

I can't get enough of his looks actually, but I can't talk.

"Can you see how much I want you, bit?"

He strokes a hand down my side. My body has never responded like this to any sort of stimuli, living or not.

The first time he tried to kiss me I was afraid and yet so excited about it, I tossed and turned all night, picturing what it would have felt like and what he would have tasted like. Well, he tastes like rain and cinnamon and mint. I'm surprised how delicious the combination is.

I lean closer. My nipples hardened like pearls. I meant to only kiss him like we did the last time, but his hand goes to my breasts, cupping one gently as he holds my face in his other hand and kisses me some more. I'm shivering, and I don't know why because I'm not one bit cold. My walls are down, my fears are gone, my reservations gone. Nothing remains but his touch and his mouth, and when he steps back to look at me—just his eyes remain. Gold-green, endless, and fiery with protectiveness, possessiveness, and lust.

There is nothing else but here, this room. The feelings. The sounds.

I'm shaken.

Chasing my breasts in and out.

What is this?

I don't know but I know I shouldn't be scared anymore.

I know that he knows I want something that could possibly lead to more. That he is the man I could see myself having more with.

I want it so bad—more more *more*—I tremble for it.

He strokes his hand down my sides.

I stand here, shivering. Already his, in most every sense. Listening to the hush of his silence and touch.

I stare at his figure in the blackness.

Among all the shadows, the dark, living substance of him. Strong, highly vibrant and alive.

I inhale and his scent pours into me.

His eyes watching me.

I've never seen a darker green, darker gold, darker look in him.

"Hold me," I whisper. His arms come around me.

Memories bubble up, of him.

Carrying boxes for me at Kelly's.

Chasing some guys who were trying to catch my attention at the cafeteria.

Looking at me when I visited the shop.

Looking at me as I left school, as I arrived at school, in the halls.

And me...thinking of him, almost too much.

Christos is looking at me now, my body still dressed but somehow my soul completely bared to him.

Christos pulls down my dress and exposes my breasts, his hand guiding it down my hips and farther down, still, to pool at my ankles. He eases my bra off, and cups me in his hand and sucks my puckered nipples, and I reach out and stroke his hardness over his slacks.

We don't kiss on the mouth. I don't know if it's to avoid any more intimacy or to enjoy the feeling of the touches— everything so intense, building and building as his fingers trail over my bare skin.

He starts kissing my mouth, all while he removes his shirt, unfastens his pants, and sheaths himself. His cock suddenly presses to my entrance —and then he's lowering me down on the carpet and pressing in.

I'm so full I can't breathe for a few seconds.

And still, I want more of what he is. What he has. Of him.

I hum deep in my throat as he moves in me, stretching me to the limit, filling me to the hilt. I feel the muscles of his back bunch up under my fingers.

He licks my throat and rises up to his elbows and watches me; his eyes are wickedly dark and sexual as he drags his hand down my sides and squeezes my ass, pulling me up to take all of him.

We're starting to move out of control, faster and faster, my nails in his back, and his mouth everywhere. He whispers something against the tip of one of my breasts, but I can't make it out over the harsh sounds of my own breathing.

He's mounting me, moving in me, and this is how I want to burn, for him to burn with me.

Raw and primal and physical.

We're moving, making mating sounds, sounds of heat and lust.

He pulls out and then back in, and I arch my back and raise my hips and roll my head side to side as the pleasure keeps building. He grabs my hips and takes what I so willingly offer, driving into me with the most delicious, measured but really hard and fast thrusts.

I take him in me and he takes me. I don't know who takes and who gives here. But Christos is taking me and giving me all I want, even as he takes my everything away from me.

He says words that are hot. Wicked. *Wicked Miss Kelly.*

It's a dance of bodies and a battle of control as we make love, one neither wants to win or lose.

Then he's coming—he's coming with me, and soon he's lying beside me, his arms around me, his mouth on mine, our breaths too fast for us to speak.

And me.

I lay here and stroke my hands over his hair, memorizing the texture. Feeling so alive every one of my senses is acute, feeling so connected I don't remember being without him.

Maybe we're not perfect, but right here, I feel perfect for this man and him for me.

It just feels as if maybe, by accident, or delusion, or some miracle, or by divine planning, we're just...right for each other.

Like I always feared, and partly hoped, we'd be.

the fall

Bryn

We didn't sleep much; neither of us seemed to need it. I get up when I smell coffee; it mixes with the smell of him on the sheets. I slip into his sweatshirt, then pad down to the kitchen. It's Sunday, so his service has the day off. It's just him, in the kitchen, with coffee brewing, making eggs.

"You're up." He smiles.

I smile back. This is the first time we wake up together to actually spend the morning with each other.

I already don't want it to be tomorrow, Monday, when I need to go back to my place and return to the hectic pacing of work.

I'm loving it, but I'm loving the off times I get to spend with Christos even more.

After eggs, toast, and the most delicious dark coffee I've ever tasted, we head to Brooklyn. I don't see him for the rest of the day because I'm busy downstairs selecting the fabrics that we will use for the first House of Sass collection.

I end up leaving to walk Milly and shoot him a text saying

I missed you. Did you have a good day?

Busy but good. See you tomorrow?
BTW missed you too.

I smile and sleep peacefully in my bed, hardly remembering why I need to set my alarm clocks at 1 a.m. when I start my routine.

I meet him early in his office the next morning, full of ideas and curious about his reactions to them.

"Do you think we could eventually expand the software to service men? I was talking to Jensen and he was complaining about his closet. And I remembered seeing this study proving men's capability of decisions diminishes with each small decision taken, which is why many successful businessmen, including yourself, always wear the same shoes, same suits, similar ties, all to simplify the small decisions, so that their big decisions regarding their multimillion-dollar businesses are taken with all the brainpower available. That's what you do," I tell him. "So with House of Sass software, even for men, the task of choosing their outfit is removed."

He leans back in his chair, interested. "Go on."

"I've also thought of offering skin-color-tone readings from our staff to suggest a complimentary skin-tone palette. The best colors that suit you. We could also have body-shape-style suggestions, suggesting the best cuts."

"Inventory my closet."

"Excuse me?"

"Take my inventory. Let's add it to the software when it's ready. Let's see what you've got for men...like me." He winks, and I smile happily and scoot down along his desk, where I'm seated, to sit a little bit closer to him.

"What do you think of our representatives visiting the homes of our clients in edgy modern mechanic outfits in blue. Kind of the one you used to wear. We're tuning up their closets, it makes sense."

He smiles, glancing at my little dress for a hot second before looking into my eyes. "I'm more for suits."

"You didn't see yourself."

He laughs and reaches for the *New York Times*, which I happen to be sitting on. "Let's stick to basics. The software sells your product, not the mechanic outfit your reps wear."

He opens the paper to continue reading what he was reading before I arrived. On the back of the paper, I spot an article about the release of *Café Society*. "Woody Allen is my favorite director," I tell him. "We should go watch that movie."

He eyes me above the top of the paper. "You like his one-liners?"

"I like everything. I feel like he's the only one doing his own thing, without chasing trends or catering to others. I like that."

"He lives just down the block."

"No."

"Yes."

"You're kidding me?"

"He plays clarinet at the Carlyle every Saturday."

"No."

"Yes," he says.

"My God! *Annie Hall* is like my favorite movie ever!"

"You want to go?" Before I can protest, he reaches around me and lifts his desk phone. "I'll get us premium seating right now."

"You're joking."

His lips curl, arrogantly so. He punches an extension, gives instruction to his assistant, then hangs up. "Yeah. Maybe I am." He turns sober, staring at me with an unreadable expression. "I guess Saturday night we'll see."

We arrive early at the Carlyle hotel and take our seats, front and center a few feet from the stage.

"You know Woody Allen is obsessed with death too? It's really obvious when you watch his movies. I watched a documentary where he talks about it. I suppose it made me feel less alone, like I wasn't the only one thinking those things."

I flush.

"Do you feel changed after your mom died?"

"Sometimes. I find myself thinking things I never would have," he answers.

"Like."

"Like people who have it bad. Like whether we have as much control of our lives as we think we do."

I look at him. "Christos, I'm having a great time this weekend."

"So am I."

We laugh and then fall sober because we were teasing but the topic maybe wasn't something to tease about. I'm really serious about him; and I think he's serious about me.

Correction: I hope, I really want him to be serious about me too.

The music starts and Woody fucking Allen takes the stage and begins playing. He looks just like he does on TV. Except real...and so close. My eyes are wide in disbelief, and I blink several times. I feel like I'm staring at a legend.

Christos's arm is around my shoulders and I lean into him with my hand on his thigh. I look at my hand, how proprietary its position is. When did I get so possessive? I look up and find him watching me with a curl of his lips.

"What?" I ask.

He smiles, silent. I'm pretty sure he won't share what he's thinking with me. He leans close to my ear so I can overhear him through the music. "You're so cute, Miss Kelly." His breath bathes warmly across my ear.

I close my eyes, then open them and exhale a shuddering breath. I'm falling faster than a ton of bricks, and into the best man's arms that could ever catch me.

What a way to fall, Bryn!

We take a walk after the show. The night is hot and dry, the city vibrant and alive.

I'm in a city with so many attractions, so much movement, so many things to do, and I wouldn't want to be anywhere else right now but...here.

I'm buzzing.

Every inch of me is buzzing.

1 a.m.

Bryn

*B*eepbeepbeepbeep.

The noise filters into my dreams. I'm instantly awake, fighting to become aware of my surroundings.

I reach out in the dark to turn off the alarm, peering at the green led lights to confirm it's 1 a.m. But rather than hit the top of the alarm, my hand hits muscled chest.

A warm male body lies next to me, and a trickle of warmth fills me as I palpate the chest beneath my hand. Oh *my*. It's real?

Christos slams his hand down on the alarm and shifts his big body—tangled between mine—in bed as he cups me by the back of the head and coaxes me closer to his chest.

"You're okay."

His lips search mine in the dark, and he kisses me.

I search his features in the dark. "I didn't dream you?"

"Nope." I make out his smile in the shadows. "But maybe I dreamed you."

"Haha."

I slide my hand up his powerful arm, clutching him closer.

"You're gorgeous," he says, running his lips along my temple as he rolls on top of me. "I'm going to give you a fuck every time these alarms ring."

"Oh God," I gasp.

"What?" he asks.

"I said...please."

He smiles as he presses his mouth to mine, crushing my mouth and pinning me down with his delicious weight as he enters me.

I hum deep in my throat.

God, it feels amazing.

"I love how you do whatever you want with my body," I pant.

"I love the way you hum when we make love, bit."

I hum again as he moves. "Do I...?" I ask distractedly. Too delirious by his way of fucking to think straight. "No," I strain out. "It just...you just feel too good. Hmmm." I hum deeper, this time more a moan.

His hips rotate, and then he pistons them forward, his arms rippling as he holds himself above me. "Hum, baby," he commands. Driving deeper. "Like that."

corner office

Bryn

I have a corner office, on the opposite corner of Christos's floor, until the store and offices are ready. The warehouse we decided upon is across the street, and I can watch from my desk as the workers get it ready for us to move in.

I'm reviewing some of the designs with Sara—who's already started to help me as my PA between dog-walking rounds—when I have a call.

"Mr. Christos," Sara says, wiggling her eyebrows.

I bite down on my lip and shoo her away, answering with a cheery, "Good morning, Mr. Christos."

"We have a problem."

I'm surprised by his tone of voice. He sounds bleak and dreary.

"What is it?" I ask, instant concern lacing my question.

"I can't get over the way you hum when you're in bed beneath me."

Pudding becomes my brain, my heart, my bones…

"Oh, that *is* a problem," I say cheekily, propping myself up on my desk and staring down at my legs as if he could see me. "Would you like me to stop by your office later today and try to brainstorm a solution?"

"No. No solutions. I want you in my office stat—I need you to do it again...and again..." he purrs silkily, "and *again* ..."

Goodness. This man! I swear my cheeks could not possibly get any redder. "I'll be right there," I say in my most professional tone, and I press my thighs together as I hang up and organize my desk. Then I leap to my feet, head to my bathroom, fix my hair, and head over to his office.

"I'm glad to see you weren't detained today," he says.

I realize he's referring to our first meeting, to which I'd arrived late. "Oh yes. No need to go to the corporate bathroom anymore when I have my own."

"That's right."

"No need to endure gray shoes and pretty shoes and tattoo fucking for fifteen minutes when I've got my own man to do."

He throws his head back and explodes in laughter.

I smile, biting my lip, waiting for him to recover. He's still smiling as his eyes fasten to mine, and his smile gradually fades. "Come here." He calls me forward.

I probably shouldn't continue to mix business with pleasure, in the office, but backing out now seems near impossible. I'm already breathing differently. My whole body feels primed for him—for now. I couldn't back out now, not even if I wanted to—a part of me needs this too much. I want it too much.

"We're in the office."

"And."

"And we're making a habit of this. A bad habit."

"Come here, bit. I'll make you feel good." There's certainty in his words, and I glance past my shoulder and notice he's removed his suit jacket. He approaches, pulling me back—flush against his body. His mouth presses to my forehead, and just that tiny contact makes me groan.

His eyes fully heavy and dilated as he slips his hand between my legs. He pets me there, rubbing my clit with his thumb.

The touch feels completely wicked—too good. He tugs the zipper of my jeans down and gives them a little yank, and before I know it, he's pulling them off my legs.

I forget to be embarrassed because he slides down my legs and leans his head in.

He breathes against my curls before his tongue snakes out. He loves kissing me there. Tasting me there.

He wedges his shoulders between my thighs and parts them with his hands, settling in perfectly between my legs. I've never been eaten out like this—no rush, only licking and tasting, probing and teasing.

I want to feel close to him. I want to feel his strength and borrow it.

My attraction to him is undeniable, the most overwhelming feeling I've ever experienced in thirty years. But now I know that I'm falling in love with him, and it exponentiates everything this guy does. It's frightening, but giving in feels liberating. I'm tired of fighting it, of being scared, of being sad and alone for years. And now here's this guy, biting my clit, lightly—and I'm constricting into a tiny ball.

I give in and for a moment, I just want it all. I want all of this man. I want to know what he wants, what he dreams, what makes him up, I want to dissect him and let him dissect me and then I want to put each other together with the wrong pieces, so one piece of him ends up in me, and some of mine end up in him.

It's an obsession, an addiction, a complete infatuation.

I press him closer, groaning.

He stands up all of a sudden, shoots me a languorous, half-mast stare, a small smirk on his lips that tells me he's very satisfied with how hot I am for him.

With a gentle but firm nudge of his feet, he toes my leg farther apart, revealing my sex a little more.

A shiver of nervousness runs through my body. He notices, smiling a crooked smile as he watches me squirm. "I don't know that I can go off with your assistant so close…"

He grabs me by the butt and boosts me up, kissing me as my sex settles against his hardness.

"You won't have any choice," he rasps wickedly.

"What is this?"

"Karma."

"Haha, really."

"It was a long time coming." He shakes his head in warning. "I'm to have my way with you daily for as long as you live."

"Christos, not against the door," I gasp, pushing at his shoulders so he lowers me.

I'm flushing, head to toe, as I head to the opposite wall.

"You're ravenous," I accuse.

"I am." His eyes glint. "And I'm only recently discovering I'm jealous too. Even of Jensen." He stalks forward, smirking. "Possessive—I'm feeling very, very possessive too." He stops before me and tilts his head as he regards me—head to toe and without an ounce of apology. "I want you in every way possible, Bryn."

I think I'm breathing a little harder than usual, but I'm trying not to. "Like what ways?"

He runs his gaze over my face, letting it linger on my throat. "Tie you up, grab you by the back of the neck, so you can hardly squirm. Have my way with you for hours."

"You're kinky."

"I'm not kinky."

"Well...do you want to gag me too? Typical guy, wanting the woman to just shut up and look pretty and take it."

"No. I enjoy that mouth of yours too much." He circles the back of my neck with his hands, as if measuring how delicate it is. "I want you undone. I want to know that you trust me. I've had enough time to fantasize about that, you understand."

"It's about trust," I say.

"It's about watching you lose control. Letting yourself get taken by me, no fear."

"You're the last man I'd trust to do anything. You're intimidating. Unpredictable. Reckless."

"You liar." He slips his fingers into mine, and my heart kicks as he tugs my arms up.

"What are you doing?" I ask breathlessly.

He secures my arms above my head with one hand, grabs his tie, and slowly unknots and slides it from under his shirt collar. Then he wraps it around my wrists.

He smiles when I squirm, and he grabs my thighs and guides my legs around his hips, then holds them locked by the ankles in one of his hands at the small of his back.

"That can't be too hard, can it?"

"I want you," I groan.

He laughs against my cheek, his lips in my ear. "You trust me, little bit?"

I groan and move my head in both yes and no directions.

I'm wet but pretending this is all a game, which I guess it is.

"If I do this, and you get ten minutes to do whatever you want with me, I get the same with you."

"That's not happening."

"Are you afraid of not having control?" I ask.

"I want my hands free to touch you."

"I bet I can make you forget all about touching me when you're being touched the way I want to touch you," I bluff.

He laughs, shaking his head, his eyes green with the sunlight streaming through the window and shining. "This is about you. Giving yourself to me."

"No, it's about you," I contradict.

"Yeah, it is too," he says, eyeing me possessively.

His eyes scan me slowly, secured for him.

I watch his face, concentrated, as he pulls off his belt and ties it at my ankles. His jaw is set at an angle, his forehead furrowed slightly in concentration. God, a man is *tying me*, what the fuck is wrong with me? And I'm secretly thrilled about it. Thrilled by the care he puts into it. He's measuring if he can fit in one finger, adjusting so that it's not too tight, not too loose.

"You've never done this before?" I ask.

He doesn't look at me as he continues fastening the belt. "I am now." He grins; his gaze darkens when our eyes meet.

"Why me?" I swallow.

"For the same reason you're here with me," he says softly.

"What's the reason? I really am here only because I've lost my mind."

"I lost that years ago." He smiles, his eyes shining again. For a moment I believe he'll tell me something tender, about our past. He doesn't. "I'm here because you give me a hard-on the kind I've never had in my fucking life. And I enjoy my hard-ons." He smiles, and then looks at me. "You look sexy like this."

"Thank you. Seeing as I don't have a mirror to check how I look, I'll have to trust you on that."

"You'll have to trust me with many things by the time we're through."

He bends his head, seizing me by the cheeks, looking into my eyes. "What's the rule on kissing."

"Kissing is…" I hesitate. "A must."

He's laughing at me with his eyes. "I thought so."

My attention falls to his lips even as I feel his attention drift down to my lips too. I start salivating at the mere idea— my pulse skipping in anticipation of his kisses. His delicious kisses.

He holds my jaw, and now that my arms and ankles are fastened, he has his hands free to run them down along the in-side of my arm, caress the sides of my breasts.

I'm breathing hard, my breasts suddenly in his hands, his breath touching the peaks of my nipples as he tugs my shirt down and pops them out of my bra.

I watch his dirty-blond head as he ducks, and I feel so full of wanting and waiting.

"I'm falling for you, Christos," I gasp.

He stops, his lips parting for a second as he raises his head.

The flash of raw emotion in his eyes nearly unravels me. I suppose it's a good thing I'm tied up, all around him, because that's all that keeps me in place as he strokes his knuckles down my cheek and curls one hand around the back of my neck, bending to tease my lips with a languorous brush of his.

"I could not be happier about that. What I feel for you is so fucking real and true, bit." He holds the back of my neck in his warm hand, meeting my eyes for a long moment.

He unfastens his pants, sheaths himself, and fills me, and as he does, he growls against my lips. I let go a noise, part hum, part groan, against his fiercely hot kisses as he holds me tied and wrapped around him. "Finally, I got you, girl. Finally, every intoxicating bit of you is mine…"

The heated possessiveness and the blatant tenderness shining in his eyes takes me to the edge—and his next thrusts takes me over it. He thrusts again, as if he knows exactly how to move, how to take me, fill me, so that there's no other thought but him, so that it's hard to believe he wasn't made to fill me…made just for me.

central park

Bryn

Mrs. Ford wants to go to Central Park with Milly on Saturday. It's a sunny but windy day, and we take a car up to the lake, then spend the afternoon by a bench, playing with Milly. She asks if I don't mind if her grandson meets us here. "It's such a lovely afternoon, I don't want to go home yet and he's visiting."

"Sure." I glance at the time. "Though it's getting late, do you mind if Sara joins you to help with Milly? I have a date tonight." I flush.

"A date. Oh goodness, go!"

"I will, once Sara's here to help you." I text Sara our location, all while Mrs. Ford grills me about my date.

"Who is he? Is it serious?"

"He's a boy I knew in high school. We recently met again and we've been going out for two weeks." I pause a moment, then admit, "It's serious. It's the most serious relationship I've ever had."

Her hand feels warm as she gives me a gentle pat on the cheek. "Don't let that one go, if he's the One. You hear?"

"I won't. I won't let him go," I promise.

I'm smiling, but then I shift in my seat, because all of a sudden it's embarrassing to admit that out loud—I suppose we're not used to expressing the feelings we feel deep inside. Not in a way that's comfortable. "You have a grandson?" I then say, switching subjects.

Her gaze instantly acquires a new, dreamlike warmth. "Yes, I do. But I really never see him. He's been in the middle of an ugly divorce and you know how those things are. Though you're very, very young, so maybe you don't?" she asks me, then rambles on with a growing frown on her face. "He stays away from the city as much as possible, and goes out on business to avoid seeing *her*." She says "her" like she'd say the most loathed word in the dictionary, and I instantly feel bad for her grandson.

"So he lives in Manhattan?"

"Yes, but he's currently quite homeless, dear," she says, sighing sadly, still looking angry and worried. "I asked him to move in with me, but he likes his space and stays at a hotel when he's in town. Seems unfair he's stuck in a hotel when his soon-to-be ex-wife has his gorgeous apartment up in West End." She purses her lips tightly and reaches down to stroke Milly in a move that seems more like petting Milly gives Mrs. Ford more comfort, almost, than the pet gives Milly.

"You know," she says, straightening slowly, "as you age, you realize how much you wish your offspring to have it better than you did, and it's rather frustrating when they don't." A new little glower wrinkles her face and sparks up her eyes.

"I'm an old-fashioned woman, I was born in Kansas! I'd have liked to see him happily married before I go."

"You're not going anywhere yet, Mrs. Ford," I warn her, serious about this—she's too much a sweetheart and she wears her years so wonderfully well. The world would be a sadder place without her, that's for sure. She just smiles and chuckles a low, raspy sound, as if glad that I want her to hang around here longer.

I'm opening my water bottle and refilling Milly's plate when I see, out of the corner of my eye, Mrs. Ford wave to someone in the distance.

"Oh, my Ian," she says under her breath, obviously excited.

I follow her line of vision to a tall, dark-haired man of around thirty heading toward us. He's quite...well, quite attractive. He's wearing a white dress shirt and formal black slacks, and he's got a serious, rather handsome face, and shiny black hair that gets ruffled by the breeze. He looks straight out of a *Suits* episode—he's even got that untouchable, workaholic air stamped all over him.

Milly's barking and leaping at him before he even reaches us, which draws out a smile from the guy.

"Bryn, this is Ian, my grandson," Mrs. Ford introduces.

He gives me a brief nod. "Bryn," he greets a little formally, then he smiles at his grandma. "Gran. How's my favorite girl doing?" he asks her in a very nice, appreciative voice, and she giggles.

"Oh, you cad. Sit down." She pulls him in next to her. I'm glad to spot Sara walking over, and I leap to my feet, too eager to head home and change for my date. "Looks like my replacement is here. I'll see you next weekend, Mrs. Ford?"

"Yes, Brynny," she says.

That's when I realize Ian is rising to full height, his dark stare fixed on Sara. Sara stops walking and gapes.

The silence becomes so awkward that I feel compelled to help Sara, for some reason, even though I have no idea what exactly it is I'm helping her with. She just seems...pale. Like she's seeing a ghost, or worse.

"Um. Ian, this is..." I begin to introduce, but he cuts me off. His tone a little different. Surprised, I think. Low, and a little questioning maybe.

"Sara. We've met." He looks at her with a brief, stiff smile, and Sara just stands there with her jaw open. That's when it hits me—I think she's found her one-night-stand man.

I hurry into the apartment to get showered and dressed, then stress about what to wear. I slip into a comfortable pair of dress pants and blouse, with a thick belt, and a long gold neck-lace. I check the time, and once I've spent 20 minutes waiting, I text him.

Are we still on for tonight?

No reply.

I grab my sketch board and try to make some drawings, then call his number and get voicemail. "Hi. Is everything okay? Call me, please, I'm worried."

Two hours pass. I stiffen every time I hear an ambulance outside, and I keep replaying the time I got a phone call to let me know my parents had passed. The news is on to ease my paranoia.

He's all right, I tell myself, fighting my subconscious fears from surfacing.

I fall asleep with my sketchpad in my hand, still dressed, with my heels on.

Sara doesn't come home until the next day.

"What happened? Did the whole city get lost last night?" I rant, worried about her too.

"We got a hotel room. We fucked, okay? End of story. He's gone again."

Wha—?

"Sara!" I say as she heads to her room, lightening up with the news. "You have his name now. Ian Ford."

"Yes. He's some mogul/magnate I couldn't resist, but it's done with." She then notices my attire. "Where are you going?"

"*Was*. I got...I got stood up. God, I can't believe he stood me up." I bite my lip and shake my head. "Something is wrong. I can feel it." I clutch my stomach.

"You're just paranoid. He'll call."

But he doesn't.

On Monday morning, I call his office. By the afternoon, when there is still no word, I head over to Christos and Co.

next day

Bryn

I cross the lobby and go directly upstairs, where his assistant is hustling to get shit done, as always.

"Is he alone?" I ask.

"Sorry. He's not." *Click, click, click,* I hear the keyboard.

"Did you tell him I called?"

She nods. *Click, click, click.*

"Why hasn't he called back?"

Click click..." He doesn't report to me, dear." *Click, click.* "I'm sure he'll call when he wants to."

God. That's it? "Will you stop typing and *look* at me."

Robertha stops typing and looks at me, her eyes wide in surprise over my outburst.

"Will he see me or not?" I demand.

Alarmed, she slowly picks up the phone, but I've had it with waiting for an ounce of his attention. The least he could have done was call—text. Send a courier. Fucking answer my dozen calls worrying about him. Obviously nothing happened to him. Obviously he hasn't crashed, gotten robbed, kidnapped, or killed. The man is fine. He's at *work,* isn't he? I start for the doors.

"He's in a meeting—" she says.

I ignore her and head straight to the double doors leading to Christos's office. I push them open.

Christos is at the long table at the far end of his office, wearing a white shirt and slacks, his jaw shadowed with three days' growth of beard—while two men stand with him, reviewing some sort of paperwork.

The relief I feel when seeing him—and confirming that yes, he is fine!!—is nearly knee-buckling. But the feeling is quickly replaced by confusion. He looks raw, a little filthy, as if he hasn't showered at all.

His eyes lift to mine when he hears me walk in—and all my hope that we could maybe work it out vanishes when I meet his eyes. They aren't cold. They aren't hot. They are simply…*sunken.*

Turbulent.

The opposite of Christos's eyes.

For the first time since I've known him, Christos looks absolutely lost. Like a man living a nightmare.

My stomach roils with my sudden concern. What happened? It's all I can think. What happened, what happened, what's wrong?

"I need to talk to you," I rasp out.

He glances sharply at the men, who look back at him expectantly. "Give us a minute," he tells the men after a moment.

Even his voice is different, low and toneless. He sounds numb.

It takes forever for the men to depart. I wait until they shut the door behind them, and then we're alone.

Aaric Christos and I.

His posture is defeated as he rakes a hand through his hair restlessly, pacing as I stand in the middle of the room, stand there like a fool who just barged into his meeting, feeling uncertain about everything.

Something is wrong. He doesn't love me. I'm so sure I start to tremble. But I want him to tell it to my face. I want him to tell me how stupid I was—how right I was in the beginning. In not wanting to get involved. Wanting to be careful.

Hell, even if I'm wrong, even a broken clock hits the right hour once a day.

He's lost interest.

I was a challenge. He's had me. Now we're *done.*

After pacing a restless circle, Christos stops at his window and his shoulders look stiff and rigid—acting like a wall between us.

It pisses me off, his silence. Seeing his hard, chiseled profile as I stress to know what he's thinking and why the fuck he's pulling away from me.

"Look at me, you son of a bitch," I say.

He turns around, one brow raised in surprise over my bad mouth. But the moment our eyes meet, the way his eyes blaze at me—as if he's living in the pits of hell—strikes me once more.

"I waited for two hours Saturday night! Then I fell asleep, still dressed, to wake up and see you hadn't bothered to call. What the fuck is wrong with you? I left you like 15 messages. You could have died! You could have been kidnapped! There could have been a fire somewhere and you could have been *in* it," I demand. My voice breaks, and an unnamable emotion etches across his face as my words register.

"God, I'm sorry, Bryn," he says. He raises his hands in the air and then he pulls them back, fisting them at his sides.

"Tell me, Aaric. *Please*." My voice breaks.

"Miranda's pregnant."

One second, two seconds, three seconds...

"What?"

I blink several times, but he still has that look on his face. The look that says he bit out the words that I just heard.

"Miranda." He drags a hand over his face, the little muscle at the back of his jaw about to break from exertion. "She's pregnant."

His ex-girlfriend is pregnant.

Aaric is going to be a father.

Aaric is going to be a father of a baby that is not mine.

My eyes begin to sting. "It's yours? I...of course it's yours, you were dating still."

I speak then. After a long, long moment. "She's pregnant with your baby."

Envy.

Jealousy.

All of those emotions that I don't like to feel, that make me feel low and worthless, are in me now.

I clutch my stomach.

"Bit."

"Don't bit me. Don't...don't come any closer."

Christos starts walking forward. I back away three steps and then stop. He stops two feet in front of me. "I never touched her after you came back. You've got to believe me," he hisses under his breath.

I meet his gaze, my chin up at an angle that belies the way I feel. Like crumpling into a stupid goddamned ball. "You know as well as I do you're not the asshole they say you are," I say. "You won't leave your child fatherless like your father did. That's not who you are."

He looks at me fiercely, as if he *needs* me to understand. "I wanted it to be you," he whispers.

"Well, it's not me. It won't be, Aaric."

I stare at his eyes and quietly beg him, *please, I love you, don't torture me anymore...*

We stay there, in silence. Both of us grappling with the news. This is nothing we planned for our future, nothing we could see coming.

"You could've at least come and talked to me. Not give me the silence treatment as if I don't deserve to know..." I whisper.

"I wanted to deal with it before I talked to you." Again, that tiny muscle flexes angrily as his fingers plunge into his hair. "What am I supposed to do, huh?" He grits out as he grabs the doctor's paper from his desk and shows me.

I think my face is wet but I don't know, all I know is the man I want to be with is having a baby with someone else.

My heart breaks when he takes my face in his hands.

He wipes my tears with his thumb.

It's something Aaric the boy would do.

A lover would do.

But he's not a boy and he's not my lover—he's nothing of mine now.

I never got to say I love you. I wish I'd said it. I wish I could now say the words leaping in my mind. *Don't leave me, choose me, have a baby with me...*

Selfish words I have no right to speak.

"Talk to me, bit," he gruffly demands, clearly fighting his own demons.

My eyes are blurry. I can hardly see him as I press my face into his warm hands. He looks at his palm, wet from my tears, and keeps drying my tears for me.

"I meant every word I told you, Bryn," he says, softly. Too softly.

"Stop. Please. I can't." I step back.

He clenches his jaw, as if I've just given him the hardest blow of all.

Rejection of his touch.

"There's no other woman for me like you. I've always known you were the girl after my heart, Bryn Kelly. Even when you didn't want to sleep with me. When you didn't want to kiss me. Even when I knew I wasn't good enough for you." He looks at me then, gold eyes like lasers, branding me. "*I meant every word I told you,*" he hisses.

"I wish you hadn't. It would be easier. I hate you…"

I drop my face to the floor.

"I hate you, Aaric."

When he touches my chin between his thumb and index finger to force me to look at him, the touch singes a path straight to the tight little knot on the left side of my chest.

I try to breathe but I can't.

"Don't be tender," I beg, my throat tight.

"I'm in hell here," he says, eyes murdering me with love.

The confession makes my eyes prickle behind my eyelids. It takes me a second to sob out loud, then react and push back from him.

"Congratulations, Aaric," I say softly. "Really," I say, trying to gather my composure.

This isn't fair to him.

This isn't fair, period.

He grinds his jaw, visibly tortured, his eyes glazed as if he's been sleepless, drinking, or simply...like he said. In hell.

"Maybe this was just ... a little vacation from realities," I say then.

"What?" he bites out.

"Our little entanglement. Just a vacation from our lives or destinies. I don't know." I shake my head, trying to make sense of all this. Unable to make sense of losing the only guy I've ever fallen for. "But we're in business and we're adults. We can at least act like it." I take another step back, gathering my courage and my pride close to me. "I'll be fine. I'll get over you."

"Come here."

"What for..."

"I just need to—" He grabs me and then we're forehead to forehead, my face in his big hands. "Tell me I'm doing the right thing," he hisses, his gaze carving into me.

"You're doing the right thing," I agree fervently, nodding, my throat aching.

He stares at me.

My eyes keep watering.

"Don't," I plead.

"Don't what?"

"You look like a guy who means to kiss me for the last time."

I pull free and swallow, putting half of the room between us. We both try to compose ourselves.

Christos's jaw is working nonstop.

"We'll be okay. You're doing the right thing," I repeat.

He nods, his jaw still locked so tight, it's a marvel he can speak.

"Bryn, I'm sorry," he says, shaking his head as if disappointed in himself.

"Don't say you're sorry. Don't be sorry. I want you to forget me. We need to both move on, Aaric."

He stares at me like I just shot us both, and I smile as if I didn't, and nod in emphasis.

"Promise me you'll forget me."

"No, bit. I promise you I never will."

I swallow.

"You have to. We have to. For your child."

"I lost my mother. I lost my daughter. And it kills me to lose you twice," he hisses angrily.

I walk over and cup his jaw, and then on impulse, I put my thumb on his lips and rise on tiptoe to kiss my thumb. Never removing it. Feeling his lips part beneath my thumb, his tongue come out to lick me.

I inhale back a sob and pull free, hearing his groan of despair and an angry, *"sonofabitch"* hiss as I walk away with my heart in pieces and my brain struggling to comprehend my new reality. The one where Aaric is with Miranda, and I need to figure out how to live with that. How to be okay with that. Without him.

her

Christos

6 weeks ago...

"**D**arling, are you ready?"

Miranda walks over, and I get to my feet and take my phone. Two things strike me then. That she's setting her hand on my chest, setting her mark, which vexes me—and the look in Bryn's eyes.

"We're done here," I say, watching Bryn closely as I pocket my phone.

"I'll wait for you in the car." She kisses my jaw, and I clench as she walks away, unable to resist noticing the way Bryn keeps her gaze fixed on me, a sheen of regret in her eyes.

I walk forward, resisting the urge to reach out.

"I'll think about it," I tell her.

"Christos."

"I said I'll think about it," I add from the door.

"Please do. I'll be back tomorrow. Same time?" she yells after me.

I smile and pause, amused and vexed that I still react to her more than I ever have to anyone. I return to the door and look at her. Small, looking hardly a year older than when I left Texas, and in my gut I know I'm in fucking trouble. "I'll make contact," I say, "if I'm interested in hearing more." I nod. "Nice to see you, Bryn."

"Nice to see you, Christos."

I walk out to the car, climb inside in silence.

I know for a fact if I let her back into my life, this could be problematic.

But I can't shake off the urge to know what she's planning.

We ride to a black-tie event in the back of the Rolls. Miranda's cloud of perfume clogging my air pipes.

"Look, if you want to sleep around with her, be discreet. If we're to have an open marriage we should always be discreet about our liaisons."

I send her a cool look that tells her that's not my thing.

But she's cool and ruthless. Understands I do it all for money. Even plan my wedding around convenience.

This is how I got to where I am.

Smart, cunning planning, no decision based on emotion.

This is why I left Austin too—there were no opportunities there for me to become what I am now.

It was easy to step into the role I did, having little emotional attachments. With my bit, however, I can never quite put a wall up between me and her. I can never quite be reasonable when it comes to her.

I still want to kiss her stupid.

Jesus.

She walks into my door, and suddenly I question everything. Who I am.

I busted my balls for years, wanting to be better. For her. For me.

I have everything I need, and more—more money than I could spend in a hundred lifetimes. And I still don't have the one thing I've wanted most in my life.

"Who is she?" Miranda asks at my silence.

What she wants to know is who she is, if she's important society-wise.

She's not really asking who she is to *me*.

"From the Kelly's department stores. The only daughter," I answer.

"Poor dear."

I stare out the window, jaw clenched because the answer, the real answer is,

My future.

And no matter how uncomfortable staring at it again is, I want it. I want her, I always will.

get dressed

Bryn

Get dressed…
    Put one foot in front of the other…
    Be open to whatever comes next…
Trust that it'll make sense in the future.

That's my motto. But I don't believe all of it. Because life has taught me. Loss is one of the things in life that stays. And some losses never make sense. Ever.

Still, I'm trying to get my life in order.

I figure if I stay busy enough, the pain will go away or at least recede. I'm working from nine to five, plus the weekends. My free time, I spend walking either alone, or with some of the dogs whose owners continue calling Sara, booking her to the limit.

I tell myself I won't think of Christos every morning, and I repeat the thought at night—but obviously I'm not listening to myself. Because he's everywhere. In House of Sass. In my email. My phone. In all of New York. In my mind and heart, the most.

"Okay, you need to start talking to me, don't shut me out," Becka said on the phone the other day.

"I can't. It's a Pandora's box I don't want to open."

"Why not?"

"For fear I'll never stop." I groan.

"Crying? Oh, Bryn."

That's my life. I've lost my parents, and my Aunt Cecile, but I have never lost someone who is still living. There is comfort in seeing him every day at work, in knowing he breathes, but while the pain is more tolerable, it is still so acute sometimes. I cannot believe this is how things will end between us.

I'm not surprised when Becka arrives one Friday afternoon. I spot her standing at the door of my apartment when I arrive home from work, and my jaw hangs open.

"Becka?"

She drops her bag when she sees me and we hug.

I ask her what she's doing here and why she isn't writing—I need her book to distract me. She says, "I can write anywhere. And that's what friends are for."

"To join the pity party?"

"That, and also to sign them up for match.com." At my displeased gesture, she hurries on, showing me my own image on her phone. "It's time to get you out and dating, Bryn. The sooner you get over him the more productive and happy you will be."

"I can't," I say.

She follows me inside. "Yes, you can."

"Hey, do I know you?" Sara asks from the door to her room.

"I'm Becka," she says.

"Oh. I'm Sara!"

"I'm also the guilty party who signed Bryn up for match.com." Becka smirks.

"Quite genius, I approve. It's been the most awful two weeks for her," she goes on saying, joining us in the living room.

"Guys. STOP. The thought of being with another guy makes me want to choke."

"You won't choke," Becka says.

"Except with dick—and only if you want to." Sara nods vehemently.

They laugh but when I don't join, Becka grabs my hand. "Your man is not yours anymore. He's having a baby, Bryn. With someone else," she says as gently as possible.

I curl up on the couch and look at the dating profile on Becka's phone screen. She used a picture of me I sent her a few months ago when I arrived in New York. Thirsty to make it. Gung-ho attitude.

I'm smiling, pointing toward the sign that says WEL-COME TO NEW YORK with a grin on my face and thirst in my eyes. That image makes me feel so beat up right now. But it reminds me of the girl I know, the one who survived the loss of her parents. It reminds me of how far I've come. "Give me that," I whisper, peering into the profile description, which is TMI and cheesy as shit, so I fix it a bit to sound more like me. Simple, young, hoping to find love and success. What every woman wants.

Except I found both, with the same man—and yet I cannot have him.

My throat constricts remembering but I swallow it back and skim the rest of my profile.

I'm not kidding myself in thinking I'll find some guy I'll fall madly in love with and have babies with—in fact, I already know the only babies I want are *his*, and that's not possible—but I need the distraction.

I can kid myself that I'm okay right now, but I don't want to be just okay.

The more distractions keep me busy, the more time will help put distance between Christos and I. Eventually, I hope to one day wake up and not have to tell myself to not think of him and then proceed to think of him all day. Miss him all day.

In a few months, my heart can feel a little less heavy, and maybe I can love again. Maybe I can find the right guy for me...again. He may not be my soul mate, but he could be someone to spend a lifetime with. Like Jensen, but who likes girls.

"Okay, so how do we do this?" I peer at the picture she uploaded on my match.com profile.

"Okay." Becka starts to show me. "Select a couple of hot or interesting-sounding guys, and give them a little wink..." she begins.

That night, I'm still scanning images of guys, trying to find at least one I can send a wink to when my phone rings.

Seeing his name on the screen and nearly having a heart attack, I answer the phone with trembling hands. "Hey." His low, deep voice runs down my ear and straight to my stupid heart.

Christos.

"Hey," I answer, blinking when I hear my alarm start buzzing on my nightstand.

I reach out to quiet it.

It's *1 a.m.*

Christos is calling me at *1 a.m.*

My chest begins to collapse when I realize this could not be a coincidence. "Christos...what are you doing?" I ask breathlessly.

"It's 1 a.m.," is all he says.

"Are you not sleeping?" I ask.

"I am. Except there's something I need to do every night at this hour."

"What?" *Set the alarm clocks?*

"Call you."

I swallow and struggle to calm my racing heart. "Really, there's no need for you to call your business partner at 1 a.m. She is perfectly fine," I assure.

"I know she is, partner. But I'm not."

Silence.

He exhales. "Guess I wanted to hear your voice. Know you were doing well."

"I'm okay," I assure. "I'm doing great. Really. I see...I guess I see the silver lining now."

Silence.

"Your son for you, for one. Or daughter. And for me... well, I guess I've realized you taught me not to be afraid to love. With your whole heart. Even if you could lose him. I'm not afraid to put myself out there again. I even signed up to match.com and may go out on a date. We'll see," I ramble. "But it's all thanks to you. You are a man who is not afraid to commit to a woman, even if she isn't the right one. You're a *good* man. You were a boy that made others pale. And you're a man that no man can compete against. You'll always be in my life in some way. You'll always be my first love. There's a reason for everything," I keep going, trying to sound positive. "I want to be your last," he hisses passionately, under his breath. "Your fucking *only*. Who's this asshole you're going out on a date with, huh?"

I'm momentarily speechless. Christos is jealous? I swallow and try to appease him. "Don't act like my brother," I chide, laughing.

He's silent, and I don't know what else to say. "Well, goodnight."

"Bit?"

Silence. "I better go. Goodnight."

My phone rings again, at 3 a.m.

I answer, my throat hurting. "Stop it. Please. The last thing I need to remember every two hours is…Stop calling me. Please."

He curses under his breath, hissing low, "I'm trying to give you space but I cannot sit here, look at the clock, and do nothing, knowing you're awake."

"Christos. Please. Go make your family and leave me be. Stop playing with my emotions like this!"

"If I'm playing with yours, you have no idea what I'm doing to mine."

At 5 a.m. I don't answer.

At 7 a.m. I cave in and answer again. "Aaric," I say, "if it's true you loved me at all, don't call me again."

I hang up firmly and then bawl like a baby.

done

Christos

4 weeks ago...

"It's not convenient for you, is it?" she asks as she slides into her bed.

"No, bit, it's not *convenient*." I look at her in bed and she looks good enough to eat. I pull up the covers. "I thought I finally had my shit together and then you come along to fuck it up. You tend to do that to me—you really are quite the Wicked Miss Kelly."

She smiles.

I cannot resist brushing my thumb over her smile.

"Goodnight, bit."

"'Night."

I drink her up, thirsty for the look of her, and force myself to go. The knowledge that she wakes herself up at night to make sure there's no fire brought my protective instincts to the forefront, and it irritates me that she has to sleep alone. That no one is there, with her, to make her feel safe.

I summon my driver with a text to my location at the curb, thinking of the ring I purchased only recently—and the fact that I don't want it in my apartment any longer.

Business has never tasted sour before.

Bryn is confusing. Reminding me of things I wanted that I thought were over now. Turns out they're not.

"To Miss Santorini's," I tell my driver as I climb into the car.

Miranda is decorating when I arrive at her Columbus Circle penthouse. I walk in in silence and pour us both whiskeys. I hand her a glass, then carry the other to the sofa, where I take a seat and invite her to sit across from me.

She does, watching me closely.

"I asked Cole to help me look at wedding locations. When you propose, I was thinking we should—" She stops babbling with a look at my expression.

"It's over, Miranda," I say.

"What?"

"It's over."

Her lips purse, and she raises her chin haughtily. "That whole block of land you want in Prospect Heights, my dad will never sell it to you if you do this."

"I know."

"You'll always be a grease monkey, Christos. My father can get you respect—"

"I'm respected well enough."

Anger flares in her eyes. "It's that tramp."

"Don't call her a tramp," I say, with low menace.

"You're not the kind of guy to walk away from business for some fancy."

I get to my feet and approach her on the couch. "Actual-ly," I say, "I'm exactly the kind of guy that's worked his whole life to recognize when it's not a fancy. I'm not going to pass something like her up."

She frowns. I lean over her on the couch.

"Tell whatever story you want to tell. Say you dumped me. That I'm no good."

"This is a terrible mistake. We made sense. We made *sense*, Christos."

"I'm sorry." I kiss her cheek. "Pick up your stuff any time. Leave your key with Clare."

"Christos, you'll hurt her," she says.

I step out of the room.

"She'll hurt you!"

Maybe.

And I don't care.

I must pursue this with Bryn.

I cannot let my one real chance with her pass.

match

Bryn

I've been getting everything ready for the launch of House of Sass; most of the details I need to handle in person, at the warehouse. I'm sore all over, but I'm putting my everything into the project. It's not only that I want to succeed, that I want the Kelly name to be attached to good things—not bad—but that I also want to prove to Christos that he was right in believing in me. Despite my busy week, thoughts of him keep coming. Not even music—my foolproof feel-good thing—can cheer me up; I seem to have developed the ability to find something mournful in every song I hear. Muscles sore and exhausted in every sense, I ask Becka for a little something to read before bed that night.

"No."

"Why?"

"'Cause I'm in the middle of my book and they're apart now."

"Ugh. Give them an HEA."

"I don't know; I mean, realistically speaking, maybe they don't get together…"

"Realistically speaking, my ass. People get together all the time."

"But not always for the right reasons," she counters. "Sometimes people stay apart for the right reasons, and that's love. Doing it for each other, not wanting the other to compromise their integrity just to be together."

"You're going to fail miserably writing love stories if you don't get these two back together, Becka. Do you hear me?!" I demand.

I head to my first date and it goes rather well. When my date walks me home, it's past midnight and my phone rings. I don't answer, even though my stomach dips in response to the sound. I spot the tall, familiar image of Christos leaning against my building entrance when I arrive.

He sees me and pushes off the wall, then plunges his hands into his pockets, and waits.

I swallow, then realize I have nothing to hide. He is not dating me anymore. I don't need to feel unfaithful because we're not together. I relax and head to the building.

"I had a great time tonight, Bryn, I hope we can do it again sometime."

"Me too."

"I really, truly enjoyed it."

I say goodbye quickly, feeling awkward knowing the man I love and need to forget is watching me.

My date leaves, and I approach the door to my building. Christos watches me through lowered eyebrows.

God, he looks delicious.

"It was one a.m. You didn't answer."

"So?"

"So I needed to see you were all right."

"I'm all right."

He stares at my clothes.

"We really need to consider that dress for the line."

"Are you criticizing my design?"

"No, I fucking like it, it's just..."

"What?"

He clenches his jaw, then leans forward. "Don't wear it out again."

"You have no right to ask that of me."

"I can't *stand* the thought of you going out."

"I can't stand the thought of you sleeping with Miranda."

"I'm not," he bites back.

I inhale sharply, then motion to the door. "Are you going to let me pass? I'm tired and I need to go to sleep."

"Get some sleep. You'll need it. I need you at 7 a.m. at the office tomorrow with a detailed list of every expense made so far."

chance

Christos

4 weeks ago...

"**I** cried when you left," she admits as we walk along Chelsea the morning after our Peasant dinner.

I brought her coffee to help with her possible hangover, and now I'm trying not to laugh at her embarrassment as we remember our goodbye from years ago. "You got my only good shirt wet," I say.

"Ohmigod. I'm sorry."

"I'm not. I didn't want it to dry." My chest feels heavier as I brush her cheek, remembering.

She reacts with a blush, accusing me, "You're a player."

I give her a look of surprise. Hell, as if I've never been called that, or worse. "I'm not. I swear I'm not."

"You totally play the game well."

God, she's adorable. I can't stop chuckling, but I sober up when I tell her, "It's never been a game with you."

"What are you doing now?" She seems genuinely confused.

I evade.

"What am I doing now?" I glance straight ahead. "Walking down memory lane, in the middle of..." I search for the street sign, "20th Street."

She smiles.

I stare at her mouth for the millionth time in what feels like the same second. I'm distracted lately, can't stop thinking of her after last night. I wanted to see her. I want to kiss her senseless. Slip my hands under her top, feel her warmth, feel her against me, force her to feel me and what she does to me.

For days, I've listened to her passionately tell me about her project, trying to keep my distance, trying to keep my head straight.

Telling myself I should say no, and instead I see her again. Asking her to do better. Wanting her to keep impressing me.

I'm impressed with her business. With her.

I want to see her, and I want to bring this vision to life.

I walk next to her now, aware of the way she drinks in the city like a new thing, like a novelty, with excitement and hope.

I don't want that hope for a future here dashed. But she's a complication in my life.

I'm giving up the plans I set for myself in the past few years, to go for the ones I had when I was young.

It takes some adjusting.

But it's like we never even said goodbye, that's how I feel when I look at her.

The night before I left Austin, she teased me, but I remember the sadness in her eyes. She cried in my arms, and it didn't feel good to hear her cry, but it felt good to hold her in my arms. I felt greedy; I wanted more. She got my only good shirt wet, and it didn't fucking matter; I never wanted it to dry. I nuzzled the top of her head and breathed three words into her hair, not because I wanted her to hear them—I actually didn't want her to—but because I needed to say them. Somewhere in her subconscious I wanted her to know she meant something.

Being with her now, vetting her more ruthlessly than I've ever vetted anyone (because I'm selfish—I want to know it all) is reminding me exactly what they meant.

This is the girl I loved and could never love.

This is my chance to do it.

lists and boxes

Bryn

The next morning, I march into the office, sleepless, angry, sad, and with the list of expenses that King Christos demanded of me.

"He's waiting for you," Robertha says when she spots me.

I swallow back my anger and frustration and walk inside, staring at anything but him as I walk forward.

I can't seem to bear it when he's near—it hurts like a bitch and nothing I do can get rid of the ache in my chest.

"Here's the list you requested. Call me if you have any questions. I need to be across the street organizing the arrival of the clothes and don't have a lot of time."

"Bryn."

I inhale and turn, meeting his penetrating gold gaze.

It's darker than usual today as he drags his hand down his face. "I'm sorry about yesterday."

"I'm sorry too. I'm not sleeping well and I suppose the launch is so close that the stress is making me moody."

"Is that it?" he asks, softly.

I force myself to nod, and the disappointment and cutting grief in his eyes makes me want to blurt out that that's not it at all. That I miss him, that I'm mad at the whole world because I don't understand why he's not with me even though I understand, I understand *perfectly*.

"Anyway, call me if you have any questions."

I head to the warehouse and get to work. I've been so busy with the launch, the crying spells are coming less frequently. I feel more in control, less as if someone else owns my destiny, more like I'm steering my own boat.

I suppose it helps to get approached by so many men on Match.com. Though I haven't agreed to any more dates as of yesterday, it helps to be reminded that I am sexy and attractive to the opposite sex.

But I still cry early in the morning and late at night, unable to grapple with the reality of having Aaric so close, having been so close to being with my soul mate and losing him in the end.

To know his kisses won't ever be mine again, his touch won't ever know me or drive me wild like it did.

"You'll get over him," Jensen says, when he meets me at the warehouse, where I keep opening boxes of the first collection.

We're busy unpacking, and sweat is coating my skin when the man haunting my dreams—my backer, my fantasy man, the love of my life and the only man I've ever loved—walks into the warehouse.

Like a king, confident, gorgeous, and *unnattainable.*

And he steals my heart from me all over again.

I spot him instantly—tall and powerful, in black slacks and a white shirt, tieless—and I'm transported twelve years ago to him arriving in his mechanic's suit to help me lug boxes at Kelly's.

My damned eyes, it seems, haven't had enough weeping, because the sense of loss I felt when my parents died, when Kelly's was taken away, and when the man I love left me comes back with a vengeance when I watch him lift one of the boxes and prop it over his shoulder only to look at me.

Dejà vú all over again.

I blink back the moisture and look away, and keep opening boxes so hard I almost cut myself.

"Hey, watch it," Jensen calls from far away, laughing.

Aaric is still standing before me, waiting, starting to scowl at me.

"You okay?" Aaric asks, his gaze deep.

"Yes."

"Good. Be careful. Where do you want these?"

I see him with the box on his shoulders and stare stupidly at him.

"You came?" I gasp.

"You needed me here, didn't you?" He raises his brow in challenge, looking cocky and a little bit more handsome than I'd like.

"Yes, but I thought you were teasing me," I counter.

"You'll know when I'm teasing you, bit." He sets the box down, moving closer, taking a lock of my hair and looking down at me. *"You'd be laughing very, very hard,"* he warns.

"Ha." I pretend not to believe him. *"You're not a funny guy."*

He tsks at that, looking disappointed at my revelation. *"Damn bad."* He looks at me thoughtfully for a moment, causing my heart to keep pounding harder and harder. *"But hey, I'm a hell of a box lugger."*

He props the box over his shoulder and chuckles as he moves it to where I've been pushing boxes across the room. I wonder what it would feel like to kiss that smile on his lips.

I swallow and avoid making eye contact. "Over by the windows. But you don't have to move them, I can just open them here and put the clothing on the racks."

Christos makes the box seem small and weightless as he lugs it across the room, then he comes back and reaches for my cutting knife and starts slicing boxes open.

I try not to look at his hands, at any part of him, even the tattoo I can see working under the white shirt he wears.

He moves effortlessly and fast, like only a guy who's actually worked with his hands for years knows how to move.

Minutes later, a dozen men appear. Christos instructs them to open the boxes and set the clothes on the racks, and though I thought Jensen, Sara, and I would take ages to finish, we're done in a few hours.

"I suppose we'll have time for the salon tomorrow night after all," Sara bemusedly tells me. She doesn't try to hide the reverent amazement on her face.

I glance at Aaric. "Thank you for helping."

He looks at me for a long moment with a twinkle in his eye, then he winks. "Still a hell of a box lugger."

I can't get away fast enough, because even his smiles hurt to see now.

1 a.m.

Christos
Present day

I sit alone in my brownstone, the city noises outside as loud as usual, my eyes on the clock on the nightstand. I sit on the edge of the bed with a drink in my hand. I picture making love to her at 1 a.m.

I remember that first night, here in my bed, when I brought her here the first time.

Setting my drink aside, I head to the bathroom to wash my face. I've got scruff I haven't bothered to shave. Reluctantly, I scoop up some shaving cream, run the razor along my jaw, then splash lotion on my face before I head for bed and sit there watching the time. Picturing her in her bed.

My little bit—

Frustration simmers in my veins.

God. What the fuck is the matter with me?

I can't let this girl go.

I am going to be a father. I lost a child once, and it nearly killed me. The grief and guilt I felt has been a regret that's weighed heavy on me for years. I still pay Leilani life support, even though we never got married, simply because that child should have been born. Should have had a father, a loving home.

I have another on the way; and still, letting go feels wrong.

As if I'm betraying her, and me. Us.

I sit in bed and remember the first time I brought her over.

How I sat in my bed at 12:58 a.m. and stroked Bryn's hair. She'd curled up on her side, her cheek on my chest, her hand close to my cock. Hell, if that didn't make things harder for me. I was ripping through my slacks and battling the urge to scoop her up, lower her down on me, and make fucking love. I'd been running her hard. Not only to teach her. But to prolong the times I saw her.

I couldn't resist teasing her, but I'd behaved. I was sick of behaving that night. My exhaustion wasn't work related, it was related to the non-stop, relentless throbbing in my gut to grab her to me, kiss her to pieces. I wanted to finish what we started on the way to my place that night. Yeah. Maybe I just didn't give a shit. Maybe all I gave a shit about was the girl with the soft brown eyes, the teasing smile, and the burning desire. I wanted to grab her, kiss her, hold her—get lost in her. I wanted her to promise me she'd never doubt my intentions again.

I sat there, fighting my battle, when I heard her breathing change. She shifted when I stroked my thumb over her lips. They parted, and the alarm started buzzing.

Her eyes opened. My chest knotted up when I saw the fear in them. Wide-eyed, scared, she looked at me, and her eyes lost the scared look as I reached out to my phone and shut off the alarm.

"1 a.m.," I said, gently.

She looked at me, starting to breathe a little better.

"You're okay," I said.

"Am I...?" she breathed.

I didn't know how to answer.

We both knew we were fucked. I knew she probably had an inkling that I wasn't going to let her go now, that I was after her—into her. Silent, I pushed my thumb into her mouth, making her lick it. She shuddered. Undone, I leaned my head down and groaned and sucked her tongue into my mouth, savoring her again.

She tensed—whispered that she shouldn't be doing this, thinking that I was with another woman maybe, but a part of me wanted her to think that. To feel the pressure of losing me, so that she could get over her resistance and open up to me.

That night, as she begged me to help her with her startup, I could see it in her eyes: she was ready for me, and fuck me if I wasn't finally the man for her.

house of sad

Bryn

I dress to kill for the launch in one of the pieces from the collection that I hope will be a bestseller: a sleek, form-fitting dress with cut shoulders and a sexy slice up the right thigh.

I cover the dark circles under my eyes, due to a lack of sleep. I waited for Christos to call last night.

He did.

And because I had been thinking of my parents, my voice wavered the moment I picked up.

"Don't cry," he husked out.

"It's okay. I just wish my parents were here," I said, and then we sat in silence for a while, and because I didn't want to spend those moments alone, instead of saying goodnight, I said, "Talk to you later?"

He called at 3 a.m. sharp, luring me from a dream of fire and screaming for them to find Christos. Christos and our child.

"Are you doing better?" he asked.

"Yes. Just nervous," I lied, speaking low into the receiver, shifting in bed with the phone to my ear, the other ear on my pillow as I stared out the window at the blinking city lights. Trying not to think of my dream, even with the lingering sense of loss in my chest. "I want to puke when I think about facing all these people tomorrow."

"This will only happen for the first time once. Make it count."

"Make me more nervous, why don't you?" I laughed, and he chuckled softly too, his voice groggy with sleep.

"Breathe, bit." He then added, sober, "It's what you wanted. Isn't it? It's what you fucking wanted, bit. It's here."

"Okay," I said, comforted by his voice.

Silence.

I love you.

"Do you have someone to kiss you goodnight now?" he asked. "Your roommate. A brother I don't know about."

"I don't have a brother." I laughed.

"Then close your eyes."

"What?"

"I'll virtually kiss you goodnight."

"*What*?" I asked, louder.

"There's no one else, right?" he dared. "So I'll have to do."

"You can't—"

"On your forehead, bit," he said.

I closed my eyes, and before he could speak, I imagined him kissing my forehead.

"Don't kiss me like a brother," I whispered, pleading, and he said, "What's left for us?"

I couldn't answer, but when I hung up I realized that to-morrow House of Sass launches, and all the joy I should be feeling has been outweighed by the awful fact of losing the only man I've ever wanted and loved.

Now, as I arrive at the warehouse with Becka and Sara in tow, both of whom are completely charmed by Jensen, I see Christos taking up the room, and my heart jolts and my pulse starts a racket.

He's in a suit, crisp and sharp as always—the one thing everyone in the room is ogling.

From the opposite side of the main floor of the warehouse that is now House of Sass, I remain motionless as my friends head inside to look at our merchandise. For three seconds, I just absorb the image of him and make love to him with my eyes.

I know his walk by memory, confident and graceful. The back of his head, his ears, his hand in one pocket, the other hanging by his sides as he greets the guests.

Miranda tries to stay by his side, putting her arm on the small of his back.

He doesn't reciprocate.

Still, I cannot move my eyes away from her hand on his back. It seems forever before my mind and my body are finally in sync, and I realize Cole is talking to me.

"Oh, hi, Cole," I greet, and for a moment I see a spark of pain and something else in his eyes, something like guilt.

"Hey, Bryn."

We exchange smiles, and then he begins to admire the clothes on display. At first I think he's going to say something, but when he doesn't, I start to wander off on my own, studying each of the pieces on display in marvel.

I absently run my fingers over the fabric of a gorgeous one-piece jumpsuit. Done in a deep charcoal fabric with a thick pearl necklace collar, it looks both edgy and classic; the fabric is so soft that it promises to be a piece that you want to wear everywhere.

It feels surreal to see my creation—a product of my mind—finally take physical form. The whole warehouse that is now the home base of House of Sass glitters tonight, its industrial style mixed with modern accents proudly displaying all of my winter collection designs along with the top designers' upcoming lines. Satisfaction fills me as I look at every piece—all of them so gorgeous, I can't imagine a woman not wanting a piece of each—and as I take it all in, a yearning for my parents to have seen this trickles over me.

Kelly's was a traditional store, and yet *this* store—their daughter's store—is for the modern woman. iPads are set up along the walls and next to each piece of display. This way, customers can easily check in on suggestions on body shapes, best colors for their skin tone, and current trends.

On these same iPads, the customers can test the software—which has all of the House of Sass collection uploaded and immediately suggests outfits currently available at the store for purchase. If they spot anything they love, customers can simply click "add to bag" or "try on" and from there, all they need to do is either meet the attendants at the dressing rooms, or meet the attendants behind the cashier, who will bring everything in their requested size to the cash register. They can add to their wishlist and email the list to themselves for future reference, and if they love the software and decide to go for their "personal style advisor" there's a free version on the iPad where they can try out not only the software's suggestions and discussing their outfits with their friends, but they can also discuss any pieces or selections with the House of Sass staff—including me.

It's exciting.

In my dreams, I always imagined having a store—maybe even like Kelly's. But I *never* imagined having something so edgy, so new and up-to-date. A Brooklyn store that caters to the entire country? It's like...wow. That is something Kelly's, with a lack of internet at the time, could never do. If only Kelly's had had those advantages, we might have survived. If we had had the same vision Aaric prodded out of me, we could have survived. Instead, Kelly's is my past, and my future...is House of Sass.

Realizing what will not be in my future, my chest starts to feel weighted down by all my emotions. Pride, disbelief, satisfaction, gratefulness...sadness.

I wander along to the next item—and it is '*the*' dress, the first dress that Aaric had made for our collection, identical to the one he gave me, which currently hangs alone in a protective plastic sleeve in my closet. I'm struggling to look at it objectively without getting my feelings involved—which is rather hard—when every hair in my arm seems to rise at attention as a large body of warmth approaches from behind.

It's amazing how *aware* I am of this man.

How aware I am of his eyes on the back of my head, of the exact position of his stance behind me.

I can feel him—every inch of his six feet-plus behind me—before I slowly turn, braced for the impact of those lovely gold-green eyes and how they always seem to snare me up and put a spell on me.

I find that this time, it's no different.

Voice...don't fail me, please... I beg myself.

"Aaric." Somehow I manage to greet him with a level voice and a smile, meeting his gaze.

He greets me with a brief nod and an embrace, and suddenly I can feel my body trembling against his.

He's smiling as he steps back, those eyes reflecting the same pride that I feel standing here in the middle of our joint venture. He stands very tall, watchful as he drinks in my reaction. "How does it feel?" he asks me.

I laugh nervously, motioning to all of the clothes hanging from the rafters in the edgiest way possible instead of on mannequins. "I wouldn't have gone all out if it weren't for you."

"No. No." He shakes his head vehemently, a tender gleam in his eyes. "This is all yours."

He reaches out to touch me but almost immediately puts his hand back in his pocket, his possessive gaze caressing me instead.

It hurts.

"How is Miranda?" I blurt. "The baby?"

"It's going well."

He nods.

"Good," I say, and force out a smile.

"And how are you?" I ask.

"All right," he says.

I nod. "I'm glad."

"Your parents would be proud of you, little bit. I'm proud of you."

I wish I could feel the pride I always imagined I would when I reached this moment. I see what we accomplished, and him before me. Gorgeous and so familiar, a part of me can't understand why I can't touch him. "Do you want to buy me out?"

His eyes widen, then he frowns. "No. This is your vision. It's nothing without you. The only reason it means more to me than business as usual is because it means something to you."

I swallow, unsure. "It's going to be hard walking to work every morning and bumping into you. Are you going to expect me to keep coming to meetings?"

"I'll ask Cole to look into things with you."

My throat constricts, and I nod.

"Well. We did it." I motion around. "I know you do this a thousand times but I'll only do it once. I don't have any more left for another." I laugh.

"You'll only have to do it once. I believe in it and you."

"Thank you. It means a lot to me." I drop my gaze. "I'm sorry I couldn't inventory your closet. You understand it would've been difficult…"

"She's not moving in with me."

I start at that, surprised. "Why?"

"Because you're everywhere."

"Please stop," I say, turning.

He catches up with me, his hand squeezing my shoulder, his voice in my ear, "I can't stop."

We face off for a moment. I'm torn between sliding my hands in his hair, kissing him senseless, while he seems to be waging his own battle, looking at his hand as if he wants it to let go of me, but it won't. He's still holding me, in his grip, his body trembling visibly.

"I can't. I can't let you go," he says, voice tortured.

"You have to stop calling me," I hiss.

His eyes are as tumultuous as I've ever seen them. He watches me as he visibly forces his fingers to start to let go of me, one by one. It hurts...the loss of his grip, so familiar to me now.

He curses under his breath and leads me outside.

I stand here, in the middle of the sidewalk, trembling.

I watch him take a deep breath before his gold eyes lock on mine, and I feel as if the Brooklyn traffic slows, like even the lights around us dim, and it's only Aaric Christos and I.

Standing a few feet away, but as far apart as when we were states apart.

"Have you given her the ring?"

He shakes his head gloomily. "I'm living a farce."

He looks at me, his eyes roiling with desire. Lust, pain, frustration. "Are you dating now?"

"What else am I supposed to do? I *love* you, Aaric," I yell.

He stares, his pupils flaring wide.

My voice cracks, but I've set it loose and now I can't stop it from pouring out. "I love you. No man has ever pushed my buttons the way you do, has ever inspired me, challenged me, ignited me like you do. What am I supposed to do?"

His mouth tightens, a tensing of his jaw that mirrors the tensing of his body, as if the battle just became more unbearable inside him. His hands fist at his sides.

"Don't go out with someone just to get back at me," he rasps.

"I'm not, we just need to let go," I whisper, pleading with him with my eyes.

He moves closer, until he's my whole world, his thigh grazing mine. "Don't," he says, his voice low and broken, his brows drawing together in an agonized expression, "be with another man. I can't stand thinking of you with anyone."

I swallow. "You're with her."

"Am I really?" he says. "I'm with another woman and I'm so fucking in love with you—I can't see past you." He narrows his eyes as he looks down at me. "All I've wanted in my life was one fucking chance with you, Bryn..." His eyes are raw with pain. "I wanted to *deserve* you. I waited years, and even decades later, I wanted to know what it was about you I found so sweet and innocent, and at the same time so damned seductive. I wanted to make you feel safe, special, I wanted to help you make your dreams come true...because you, Bryn, you were my own dream coming true for me. The family I wanted...I wanted to give it to us *both*. You and me. Our kids would have no grandparents but they'd have two parents who loved them and were madly in love with each other..."

"Stop."

"I love that when you needed, you came to me. That I was the one you trusted with this dream. I told myself this was our time. Maybe not ideal, but that this man I am now, that this is the man you were waiting for. And now this," he grates. "Tell me how to let you go when every day all I look forward to is fucking seeing you. Tell me how to let you go when I look in your eyes and see I hurt you." He looks at me, wondering, frustrated.

"Then choose me," I breathe.

His gaze flickers in surprise.

"Choose me, Aaric. I wanted you to do the right thing, but I don't even know what the right thing is anymore. I want you to choose me. I want to love you and love your son or daughter even if it's someone else's. I want to be your girl and I want to be by your side. I want you like I want Manhattan. House of Sass. Like I want to have called my parents that night. We have enough regrets, Aaric. Can you tell me you won't have none if we do this?"

His eyes darken.

"I know you want to be the best father possible, but you can. You can be happy, you don't have to sacrifice us to be the best dad, we can still do this, we can have an us. Just not if you marry her. This is our last chance, Aaric."

He drags a hand over his face, his jaw tight, his eyes flashing fire. "Do you realize my child will grow up without a father? Would you wish that on my kid?"

"You can be there! Can't you see?"

I start to cry, and I drop my head and sniffle quietly because I'm so undone. Christos's energy is tumultuous as he somehow manages to shift even closer, shielding me from the onlookers.

He lifts his hand and when he cups my cheek, I turn my head instinctively, the touch so familiar, so achingly familiar, the tears stream a little faster. He draws me gently into the back of his car, parked right in front of the warehouse.

He shuts the door behind us and, as if he needs the distance, sits right across from me as I keep crying. He's looking out the window, his eyes red.

He scrapes his hand down his jaw. He doesn't seem to be breathing, his jaw set, his posture closed off and tight. It seems to be costing him everything to keep himself on a leash, because he doesn't even speak.

We stay like that for a while, sitting with our prides, our reality, and holding onto our love as tightly as we need.

"Loving you fucking hurts," I accuse, trying to stop crying.

He reaches out to take my shoulders, his forehead to mine—his eyes livid with pain. "You think this is easy for me?" He grabs my face, frustrated and trembling, his voice a hiss. "You're the only thing that makes me feel really alive. I'm not living without you. I'm just here—a money machine, all for what. Huh? When I die tomorrow who would've cared for me, really, other than my brother? If I'm in some accident, if something happens to me, who will make me cling to life? Who will make me want to stay here?"

"Stop it, Christos. You'll have your son, or your daughter."

"But I won't have *you*, love." He takes my chin and looks at me, at my whole face, and says, "If I have joint custody, would you be there for my child? As if it were yours?"

"I'd love it as hard as I love you," I sniff, my tears streaming down my cheeks as he rubs them with the pads of his thumb. "I'm sick of feeling like it's wrong to love you because you're not mine to love."

"I love you," he says. "I want a family, and I want it with you." His eyes gleam mercilessly as he wipes the rest of my tears. "It kills me to hurt you when that's the last thing I've ever wanted to do. It kills me to let you go because I fucking can't let you go. I'm choosing you. It's always been you. Will you choose me too? Choose me and my child too?"

I swallow, and his eyes have all of this tenderness inside them that I can barely breathe. "Are you certain?" I ask, sucking back a breath.

"I'm certain. I have this disjointed idea of being the kind of father I never had. Maybe I even don't believe I deserve to have a family, a real family, like I'd have with you because I failed Leilani and my daughter once." He cups my face and sets his forehead on mine, inhaling me. "Maybe why I was settling for Miranda in the first place. Something surface. Nothing real." He eases back, and I keep getting tears, even though the emotion behind them is woefully different than when I started crying. Because Christos looks all raw, all open, all mine as he keeps the back of my neck in his hand and pins me down with the most glorious eyes.

"We sometimes don't get the family we choose, even the kids we have, or how they sometimes come. But you choose who you marry. Who you spend your life with," he says, trailing off.

There's silence between us, my heart pounding madly as I wonder if we'll make it work. If Miranda will let him go. Give him joint custody. If he'll really let me take care of his kid and let me love him like one of mine. Like we would also love ours, his and mine.

We seem to eye each other hungrily from across the car.

I wonder where we stand.

A conversation away from him being mine to hold again, mine to touch again, to love as hard as I want to and can.

"Do you want to take this talk elsewhere?" he asks softly, watching me. "Preferably after I've had a word with Miranda?"

I smile shakily, and God, I've never been so eager to send him to Miranda, and I nod so fast I almost get dizzy as I wipe away the moisture from my face, and I quickly get out of the car.

I hear Christos step out of the car as Cole and Miranda walk forward.

"Where the fuck were you two? The evening is a huge success and nobody can find you two!" Cole demands.

Miranda and I lock eyes, and she lifts her nose up in the air, gloating. Her eyes saying, *who got him in the end, little bitch?*

"Hello, Miranda," I say politely, keeping my gaze away from Aaric as he walks up behind me, and that's when I notice Cole's shoes.

My eyes widen in recognition, and as I pull my gaze up, it snags on the ankle of the woman's leg standing beside him. On the ink tattoo on Miranda's ankle.

"Nice shoes," I say as I look up at Cole, and then at Miranda, a little bit too stunned by the snotty look she keeps wearing. "Nice tattoo, Miranda. I have a feeling I've seen it before. Maybe at the corporate restroom of Christos and Co." I smile at her as genuinely as I can, and I look at Christos, who's wearing a puzzled frown. And then something flickers, and I see it in his eyes.

I walk away, not glancing back.

"You two. We need to talk," I hear Christos growl behind me.

choice

Christos
Present day

"I'm not marrying you to pretend a happy life. That's not what I want to teach my child. I will be there for this child, regardless. As an uncle, or as a father," I tell Miranda.

Miranda purses her lips, too proud to say a word to me.

"I was about to let the girl of my dreams go. Jesus!" I growl. She tilts her chin up, and I glare down at her before I turn to look at my younger brother. "And you. You *mother-fucker*."

"Come on, Aaric. You didn't love her. She's insisting the kid's yours because she's got this idea of you being better than I am. A better father figure. More responsible. She knows you want a family, and I don't."

"Yeah, well now you might get one. Fucker."

I pace, still reeling, before I spin around to point a warning finger at him. "Don't you ever—*ever*—fuck in my corporate bathroom again. Lock your damn office door—or take it somewhere else. As long as I pay the rent, you screw around elsewhere." I glare at them both, then move around to watch the spot where Bryn disappeared.

"If it's mine, I'll be the father you were to me. The damn best," Cole says behind me.

I shoot him my blackest look. "If you don't, I'll personally make sure that you do."

"Miranda, hell, I know I'm a bit more *c'est la vie* than Aaric, but even if Aaric is the biological father...I can—well, be there for the stepfather role."

I glance at Miranda as Cole waits for her reply, and she tips her chin up, raises out her left hand, and points at her empty ring finger.

I keep staring out the window, unable to see Bryn, remembering how fast her tears streamed, how warm they felt falling into my palms.

Choose me.

Did I ever not choose her? Can I ever not choose her?

Damn me, did I ever have a choice of anything other than her?

always

Bryn

I head home and replay the scene over and over in my head, and not only the moment when I realized my secret-restroom lovers were Cole and Miranda. No. Not that mind-boggling, what-the-ever-living-fuck moment.

Also, before that.

Years before that.

Wondering when I sat in the back of his car, fighting for Christos, why I couldn't have been braver before he even met Miranda, so that things would have not come to be this complicated. Wondering what would have happened if I hadn't been afraid of falling for Aaric years ago. Wondering if I could have rescued us from heartbreak, like I've wondered for years what would have happened if I'd called my parents that night.

I'm retracing all the steps I have taken—and all the steps that led me here—trying to figure out where I went wrong, which step is preventing me from achieving the one outcome I want and seem to be waiting on bated breath for. The outcome where Christos and I finally have a chance to be together.

I'm circling it all in my head like you'd replay a shocking moment or a favorite one, remembering our times even while fully aware that there is no changing what is now, no changing those past moments, aware that I only have choices in my future ones, and perhaps *that* is not even possible at all, when I get a call from Cole.

"Hey. Just wanted to call and say I'm sorry."

I don't know how to reply. I'm surprised that he's calling me considering he has more important things to talk about with his brother.

"I planned to come through," he continues.

"Why are you apologizing to me?" I ask, completely baffled.

"Because no one should be without the woman he loves."

"You love Miranda," I say when it dawns on me.

"I meant my brother."

"Oh."

"You do love him too. Don't you?"

"Is he all right?" I clutch the receiver tighter and hold my breath while I wait for his answer.

"Ha. Better than ever. He said I did him a favor. I should be a good dad like he was to me."

"So it's yours?"

"I suspect it is. But we'll make sure. Even then..." he trails off.

"What?"

"Nothing." He repeats, "You do love my brother, don't you?"

"Always," I croak.

"Good. I hope you two spend the rest of your lives proving it to each other."

He hangs up, leaving me buzzing in hope over his words as Sara texts.

Are you okay? You left and everyone was gone but Christos—he said he was staying until all the guests were gone. Becka and I offered to help.

Yes, it's just…I'm okay, I text.

This whole thing with the baby has really made me realize how deeply, how completely I love him. I just want it all, *him* in any way, even with baggage and with anything else.

I curl my legs underneath me as I sit on the couch and stare at Christos's contact.

I want to thank him for staying to make sure things went smoothly, for safekeeping my business for me when I should have maybe stayed too.

I lost it tonight. What I asked of him was selfish of me to ask, but I keep thinking: *this is one chance.*

We have just this one *chance.*

And he chose me. He looked at me and those eyes were clearly saying, he chooses *me*.

Oh god. Nervous about how his talk with Miranda will go, I stare at my phone. I want to call him and ask how he is, but I also want to give him space.

I need to walk. Clear my head. So I head to Washington Square Park. It's isolated at night, and all lit up. The arch, the fountain, the water, it always makes me feel better. At 11 a.m. the dog park is full of dogs, but tonight at 11 p.m. it's vacant.

"Pretty nice all lit up. Isn't it?"

I flip around, startled to see Aaric standing there. As real as real gets, and as gorgeous as he was an hour ago.

"What are you doing here? How did you find me?" I ask, breathless.

He raises his hand. "Find my friends." He shows me his phone. "Or should I say, Find the love of my life."

"You don't believe in that."

"Yes, I do. But I found her too early. Too easy. Maybe sooner than she was ready. Sooner than I was ready."

There's a soft sound—the sound of me sharply inhaling my breath as he comes to stand next to me. To watch the fountain, next to me.

The familiar feel of his body heat envelops me. It fills me with such acute longing I need to bite down desperately on my lips while I try to remember to breathe.

"She's getting tested as soon as she can," he says.

My heart is starting to pound as he reaches out to hook his index finger with mine. He runs his thumb along my hand, his voice low and tender.

"You were right. This has been so hard because the truth I've been trying to accept is wrong. It doesn't matter if I have a child with someone else as long as I want you, love you.

"This issue with Miranda has felt so painful because it's wrong. Because we could do this, Bryn. You and I. Because this is our only second chance. Our last chance." He takes me by the shoulders and turns me around to face him—his eyes a dark, vivid gold and raw with emotion.

"Anything keeping me away from you is wrong. My fears or yours. My desires for a family even when you can give me one. We sometimes don't get the family we choose, even the kids we have, or how they sometimes come. But you choose who you marry. Who you spend your life with. And I very," he emphasizes meaningfully, "desperately want it to be you."

He shakes his head slowly. "No family can be happy if the father is miserable. I would want my child to be proud of me, knowing I did the right thing and not hurt the girl I've always loved." He cups my face. "I want a family. I want it with you. The woman I lo—"

Anxious, I quiet him with my finger, pressing it to his lips. Then I quickly, almost frantically, rise up on tiptoe, pressing my mouth to my thumb and kissing it. I drop my thumb, and then I'm kissing him because in the midst of all the *what ifs*, sometimes you need to make a choice.

He takes control and lifts me up, kissing me thoroughly.

A couple of tears slip out, sliding down my cheeks as I smile against his mouth. "Don't cry," he says.

"I'm happy. They're happy tears."

"Then I won't mind seeing more of that."

A tender look sweeps into his eyes as he drinks me in, dries my eyes as if he won't ever have me cry again, and he leans down and kisses me some more.

"You look gorgeous." He eyes my dress, when he eases back to let me catch a breath.

"This old thing?" I tease.

He smiles.

"Amazing what the right clothes do for a woman even when she feels like shit," I admit.

"Amazing what the right woman does for a man even when things go to shit."

He brushes my mouth, hungry, as he nuzzles me.

"Always had a thing for your nose," I breathe.

"Really."

"Hmm. Lots of character." I nuzzle him.

"Big as shit."

"Yes."

"All the more to smell you better."

I laugh and snuggle into him. "You're all big as shit, it's perfect on your face." I stop to touch his face. "I love your face."

Tenderness, it's wild and free and raw and primal, and it's all in his kiss as he nuzzles my nose with his, melting me before his lips crush mine sort of proprietary, sort of fierce, sort of possessive, sort of exquisitely.

He boosts me up by the butt and sets me down on the fountain ledge, bringing me to his eyelevel.

I slip my arms around his neck, and he holds me by the waist. "For a while I've been all business. After I lost my mother. I was good at it. I convinced myself that if you'd have gone for me, you would have, long ago—so I never came back. I was good at business, and that was that. I thought I didn't need more. I do." He slides his hand into the back of my neck, his grip possessive on my nape as he squeezes gently, his gaze carving into me. "I want, need more. *You.* Your acceptance, your love. Your smiles, your kindness, your sweetness. Mine. For *me.*"

I nod so fast I get dizzy, and he chuckles as he boosts me down. We start to walk along the park.

He looks at me as if he doesn't plan to forget a single feature of my face.

We look at each other as if for the first time.

"Let's have a do-over," he says, tugging me close.

"No." I shake my head, pressing my cheek to his chest. "I don't want to have missed a thing."

"Then let's not miss a thing of what's coming."

He looks down at me and brushes my lips with his thumb. "Babies."

I nod.

"Marriage."

I nod.

"Considering I'm marrying you in City Hall as fast as I can...can I at least have your name?"

I laugh, cheeks burning.

"Bryn."

"Bryn. I'm Aaric," he says, cupping my cheek in one big hand and bringing his eyes to look deep into mine, giving me the most devastating grin. "Bryn, I see my future in your eyes."

DEAR READERS,

Thanks so much for picking up *Tycoon*. I hope you enjoyed Christos and Bryn's story as much as I did writing it. And most definitely, yes! Sara and Ian are next! ☺

XOXO,

Katy

acknowledgments

Although writing is a personal thing and sometimes quite a lonely profession, publishing is a whole other beast, and I couldn't do it without the help and support of my amazing team. I'm grateful to you all.

To my family, I love you!

Thank you Amy and everyone at Jane Rotrosen Agency!

Thank you CeCe, Lisa, Anita, Nina, Angie, Monica, Kati and Kim.

Thank you Nina, Jenn, and everyone at Social Butterfly PR…

Thank you Melissa,

Gel,

S&S Audio,

and my fabulous foreign publishers.

Special thanks to Sara at Okay Creations for the beautiful cover

And to Wong Sim and Chad Hurst for the kickass image.

Thank you Julie for formatting,

to bloggers for sharing and supporting my work throughout the years, and readers~ I'm truly blessed to have such an enthusiastic, cool crowd of people to share my books with. You are the greatest.

Katy

about

New York Times, USA Today, and Wall Street Journal bestselling author Katy Evans is the author of the Real, Manwhore, and White House series. She lives with her husband, two kids, and their beloved dogs. To find out more about her or her books, visit her pages. She'd love to hear from you..

Website:
www.katyevans.net

Facebook:
https://www.facebook.com/AuthorKatyEvans

Twitter:
@authorkatyevans

Sign up for Katy's newsletter:
http://www.katyevans.net/newsletter/

titles by
katy evans

TYCOON

White House series:
MR. PRESIDENT
COMMANDER IN CHIEF

Manwhore series:
MANWHORE
MANWHORE +1
MS. MANWHORE
LADIES' MAN
WOMANIZER

Real series:
REAL
MINE
REMY
ROGUE
RIPPED
LEGEND

CPSIA information can be obtained
at www.ICGtesting.com
Printed in the USA
BVOW06s0730020717
488311BV00017B/1107/P